NIXON IN LOVE

A HISTORICAL NOVEL

Wayne Soini

NIXON IN LOVE
A HISTORICAL NOVEL

iUniverse books may be ordered through booksellers or by contacting:

iUniverse
1663 Liberty Drive
Bloomington, IN 47403
www.iuniverse.com
1-800-Authors (1-800-288-4677)

ISBN: 978-1-4917-9327-5 (sc)
ISBN: 978-1-4917-9328-2 (hc)
ISBN: 978-1-4917-9329-9 (e)

Library of Congress Control Number: 2016905224

Print information available on the last page.

iUniverse rev. date: 4/11/2016

Dedication

To
"Huh?"
the last line of *The Maltese Falcon*,
a movie from the era of
The Dark Tower

CHAPTER ONE

The Sound Mirror

Semi Begun was on Dick Nixon's mind.

"That's his real name," Dick's fast-talking, fast-eating new best friend, Ira, had told Dick at a trade association meeting the previous week.

"Great inventor, the German Edison," Ira said, speaking between bites of a ham sandwich he'd grabbed up from the big buffet set-up at the glitzy Los Angeles Biltmore, "Born in Danzig. Educated in Berlin. A genius. Lives in Cleveland now, in the home of the brave and the land of the free."

"What is his 'Sound Mirror' and how would it help my business?" Dick asked. *Get to the point.* Dick, a new lawyer, was also the new president of a new orange juice company attending "Inventions for Business 1938," his first trade association meeting. However, "Inventions for Business 1938" was looking more and more each minute like a trap set by salesmen to catch new clients.

At Dick's question, after chewing and swallowing the last morsel of his ham sandwich, Ira's mouth slipped into high gear.

"In five different ways, every day, count them," Ira said. He was wearing a blue-and-white-striped seersucker suit and a red bow tie. Ira formed his hands into all sorts of gestures while frequently hitting Dick on the shoulder, a most unwelcome contact Dick shrank from. Dick could only think of the greasy ham sandwich so recently in Ira's hands. "One, it's your secretary, around to take notes twenty-four, seven. No powder-room breaks for this baby. Two, you can dictate your letters just as fast as you care to, then replay it on slow speed as many times as it takes for Miss Bliss to transcribe. Three, you can talk on the phone and get down your end of any conversation. Four, you can can speeches – get it, can can? -- for the machine to deliver, your own little ambassador of yourself. Fifth, wiretapping is illegal, don't get me wrong, but you could use it in secret, under your desk and, *voilà*, under there you find a perfect, literal transcript of everything everybody said at your office meeting. Or whatever."

"Wow," Dick said, his dark, beady eyes lighting up. "How much is this thing?"

Ira went into a frenzy, as if he were having a fit or trying out for the Wizard of Oz.

"The Sound Mirror? Why, the price of Semi Begun's – accept no substitute, Semi Begun's, I say – for Semi Begun's original, authentic, guaranteed-by-me-personally genuine magnetic tape recorder -- available commercially for the first time at this convention in San Francisco—"

"Los Angeles," Dick said, sourly. "The price?"

"Quite right, available commercially for the first time at this convention right here in Los Angeles – I say, for the first time anywhere – is intrinsically priceless."

"No price?"

"Beyond value," Ira said, his eyes gleaming like a fanatic now. "However, anything made in this greatest of all commercial democracies where any man, woman or child may purchase a Coca-Cola for the very same nickel can be had for a price. Even the wonders of science crafted by the greatest marvel-makers of all time, Semi Begun and the workers of the Brush Development Company of Cleveland, Ohio, the U.S. of A."

"The price," Dick said.

"You, sir, look like I can trust you. The price I will give you I must whisper into your ear. I not only include the first-time-buyer's discount, the discount for the demonstration model I brought with me, its case included, and the discount for cash. Tell no one," Ira said in prelude, then whispered a figure into Dick's ear.

Jesus.

"Give me your card, Ira," Dick said. *Way too expensive.*

Now, one week later, on his way to church to audition for *The Dark Tower*, Dick thought as he drove slowly along in his Chevy how much he still wished that he owned a Sound Mirror. It would be like magic. Dick chuckled for the hundredth time imagining recording his father, and showing the old man how contradictory his opinions were. Dick would not have to cross the line of criticizing or arguing with Dad – a rule Dick made and kept religiously – Dick held "honor thy father" to mean "let the old man figure out his own mistakes" – Dick would only have to play the recorder back to Dad. But would Dad even hear himself? There was the rub that sapped all the fun out of it. Dad was going deaf as a post. Dick, on the other hand, was beginning to hear everything more acutely than when he'd been in school. Even in law school, Dick had been too much the speaker, too little the listener. He was changing, he was growing up. How great it would be to rehearse a speech, or prepare for trial by speaking into one of Semi Begun's machines. Semi Begun. One day Dick must buy a Sound Mirror. One day.

CHAPTER TWO

Reverie where bees are few

I was riding my bike but I was actually at the top of the Wheel of Fortune. Never better, never happier, four o'clock, Eastern Standard Time, I was done delivering pizza for the day, plus there was no function to bar-tend that night and the Central Square Do-Nut Shoppe did not expect me until tomorrow. And, best of all, ladies and gentlemen, I was free of school, free of school, thank God Almighty, free of school. With my final final (I loved saying that) in *Watergate in American Memory* (a course I dubbed "Amnesiagate") I had -- ta-DA -- earned my baccalaureate. I had sold my final final books for a couple hundred dollars. Yay. I had verified at the Bursar's office, conveniently located next to the bank, that I did not owe another farthing for overdue books, forgotten lab fees or lost gym towels. Double yay. Nothing stood between me and my Harvard degree now but three weeks' time and best of all, best of all, I made the stretch run all by myself, no thanks to Dad. Triple yay.

Not that I ever stopped hearing from Dad.

Last night, in fact, as recently as last night, Dad called and, with no greeting or prelude, nothing, asked, "You change your mind, son?" and when I said no, he hung up. No surprise. I say, no surprise. Hey, if I heard once that I was the son, grandson and great-grandson of great lawyers, I heard it a hundred times. He was a repeater, Dad was. Dad had a wish carved in stone, the cold and indifferent stone that served him in lieu of a warm heart. That wish I never recall not knowing. That wish was that his only child, son and heir – to-wit, me -- go to law school and become a lawyer, any kind of lawyer, even a poor, pathetic, eyes-glazed-over, indifferent lawyer. I was not a good enough advocate to persuade my own father otherwise and you'd think that would have been enough of a clue that I was not cut out to be a lawyer arguing with other lawyers but, no. As his last and final pressure, Dad shut the water off; for my last semester, without notice, he sent no tuition, no allowance, no birthday check, no bonuses, and no holiday gifts. What did it mean, finally? It only meant that I need not worry about graduation day weather for my family's sake. Dad and Mom would be out yachting in Long Island Sound. Dare I cheer? You bet I cheer. Quadruple yay.

As I sped down JFK Street before turning left on Memorial Drive on my way home to East Cambridge, I would have felt more joy in sheer existence had three worries not popped into my head simultaneously. Worry Number One: I was broke. Worry Number Two: I had barred Arlene from my apartment, Arlene, the love of my life, who shares not only my love of history, of movies, of literature, of Van Gogh, but is also a gifted researcher who knows all of my erogenous zones. "It's my author's studio," I told her when I announced my edict last week. "A workplace." Worry Number Three: my novel stood incomplete. All three problems were one problem, of course, one that I might solve only by finishing my novel. I simply had to finish my novel.

I was 80 pages along in the first draft of my projected 500-page novel entitled *Downriver, A Novel of Young Man Lincoln.* Lincoln's flatboat was barely out of the Sangamon, on the Ohio River heading west. I calculated that at my current rate of a page every five-and-one-half days, the novel would be ready to publish in eight years unless I had to make a second draft, which would extend the time needed. If I quit some of my jobs, I'd make quicker progress but then I might be evicted for non-payment of rent. I refused to let anybody else support me now that school was over. Oh, sure, I had a Plan B: I would teach kids history, make a living and make a difference in some lives that way. But the novel, oh, the novel, I wanted to write a novel and make a million dollars, show my Dad what I was made of and get my picture in the *New York Times Book Review* hugging Arlene. Maybe I could cut down on sleep time. I kind of knew what I was doing. They say to write the sort of novel you like to read and I read historical fiction. They say write about what you know and I had majored in American History -- which is largely the Civil War which is, largely, Abraham Lincoln. However, on most nights my mind drifted to Arlene. Other nights, working nights, you know what I discovered? Snobs abounding to whom I was invisible, a born loser necessary solely to link their mouths to a drink or a donut or pizza. They looked not at me but through me, or in back of me, or down, seeking pizza prices, donut varieties or bottle labels. Even my fellow donut jockeys, pizza parlor crew-mates and booze-tenders offered little support.

I, a nobody, a *schlemiel*, attempted some connection. At a slow moment between deliveries at the pizza place, I had asked blue-eyed Cinda, "short for Cinderella," in her big-but-still-too-tight jeans and purple hair, the question, "When was World War Two?"

Cinda asked me first, had there really been two.

"I thought it could be a trick question," she said, smiling as if she had been shrewd. Then she guessed, "1776," and added, "Richard Nixon," and smiled yet more broadly.

"He was in it, right?" Cinda asked.

"He was," I said, nodding. "You got that right." Richard Nixon had been in World War Two, truly. Cinda was right.

"Yay," she said in a way too childlike for an eighteen-year-old.

The truths I found around me were altogether stranger than any fiction. At least the fiction I wrote seemed *plausible.* The life that I was living seemed as off-track as the wobbly wheel on the proverbial ox-cart. *Dukkha, dukkha, dukkha,* an accident waiting to happen.

For relief, I turned to look at and to see, really see the sparkle of sunlight on the Charles on my right. It felt so good. I was always a sucker for sparkling, squiggling water in nature or in paintings. Happiness regained, I swore by Arlene that when I published my novel I'd buy us a large squiggly-watered harbor scene by one of the Impressionists. I'd no sooner turned back from the river to the road, pedaling just a little bit faster than somebody else expected, when I was hit by a big truck.

CHAPTER THREE

The Hospital without George C. Scott

Although the truck was big – that much I myself vouch for -- it was slow – very fortunately slow -- *and* its driver braked sharply just as I went down, doubtless saving my life. The good driver spoiled a perfect score, however, by thereafter "departing the scene at high speed," as stated in the police report I read later. Hit and run. I bet he was a Red Sox fan. No matter, I survived. I woke up in the hospital, you know, the warehouse where the inventory crew wear white coats and monitor and water their stock regularly, nurses, porters, techs, doctors milling and circulating to be sure that nobody was lights out who was supposed to be awake, and that people ate dry toast, skimmed milk, took their pills and pooped regularly. You couldn't pay me enough to work in a hospital. We need doctors, though, just like we need immigrants to take all the bad jobs that can't be filled by novelists or actors. Doctors are idolized, beatified even. At least my father was not a doctor.

Ever since a tonsillectomy that went haywire back when I was ten, I have always hated being in the hands of the doctors so that only happened when I had just been hit by a truck. I kept my hatred to myself and, like Nixon, made and kept adding to my enemies' list. You know what I especially hated? I hated it whenever they said, in some words, usually in jargon, something like I could die. I always wanted to shout back, "*You* could die!" I never, ever did but I always wanted to. I felt more emotion than I showed.

Anyhow, I'm sure that I was told, forgot, was told again, forgot again, and was told again and again by nurses and doctors on several shifts until what they kept repeating stuck memorably in my head: that I had been a) in an accident, b) my right leg was broken, c) the doctors had done surgery and reset it in a cast, d) I'd also suffered a concussion but e) there was no internal bleeding and f) my brain was not swelling, g) all good signs, except that g) I now had a raging secondary infection from long scratches on my left leg – (Me: "The itchy one?"; Doctor: "Yes, the itchy one") --that h) required monitoring and attention or i) I could die. No, *you* could die.

"When can I go home?" I asked the doctor, who was not George C. Scott but all big-eyed and bird-beaked. I thought of Dr. T. J. Eckleburg and Old Owl Eyes in F. Scott Fitzgerald's *The Great Gatsby.*

"Dr. Patel," he said, offering his hand to shake.

I was busy scratching my right leg, upper thigh.

Noting my hands, Dr. Patel then said, "Don't scratch. The nurse can apply lotion."

I don't know why but that sounded funny and I laughed. But when the laugh was over, I still itched.

"It's burning, like it's on fire, Doctor," I said. My father said to me in my own younger and more vulnerable years: get a young doctor and an old lawyer. Yes, advice I'd been turning over in my mind ever since. I had an old doctor. Dr. Patel may have had black hair once, but he was as bald as Gandhi in old age now. To make things perfect, I wanted the youngest member of the Massachusetts bar to sue my hit-and-run driver.

"Lotion," Dr. Patel said, his beak bobbing, ever more the reincarnated owl.

"When can I go home?" I repeated. I was surprised to miss my sagging mattress and unmade bed, clothes strewn about, dusty piles of books and a sinkful of dishes crawling with critters. However, in my *pied a terre* not a machine on wheels was in sight, I wore actual shoes even if the heels were slanty, rather than slippers, and its ambience was donuts, pizza and beer, rather than Lysol, urine and steamed broccoli. Also, of course – there I was monarch of all I surveyed. Here, I was under an Owl's thumb.

"We'll see. You have a secondary infection, you're on antibiotics," the Owl said.

Oh. Sometimes you can only sit and stare, stunned to silence before the grinding gears of fate, nature, history, and hospitals.

"A few days, right? I can't miss work," I said, probing, thinking, *get me out of here, they are going to kill me, I almost died when I was ten. Aiiiii.*

"Not days, at least a week, maybe several," the Owl said. "Why not start a project? You're a student, right?"

"I was. I work. I've got three jobs."

"Arlene called them all."

"Arlene was here?"

"She was here night and day for your first forty-eight hours."

I love answers. I love Arlene.

"What did she tell them?"

"You'll have to ask her. We argued with her to go home and get some rest. She was here until this morning and she said she'd be back soon."

"Wow," I said.

"Oh, yes, she also called your parents, and she told me to tell you that she told them you would be fine and that they need not come here to be with you."

"Double wow."

"Right, double wow," Dr. Patel said, smiling now with that upper curled lip that showed teeth. "She sounds like a keeper."

So, just when I was graduating, self-supporting and starting to believe that most questions actually have answers, I'm on my back, itching, awaiting lotion, wearing a night-gown without a back in a world where other people were doing my calls and keeping my life from totally falling apart. I detected something familiar. I was in Novel-land, where really good questions never have really good answers. That was the reality all around me.

CHAPTER FOUR

Enter Nixon

"Look at this," Arlene said, her first words after our hugging and kissing exercises and all the spontaneous squeezing, pressing, caressing missed-you signals that we could invent on the spot. No need to describe love to you, reader, you've been there, done that. It never seems to grow old, though. Arlene was my Rembrandt smudge made flesh, Mozart notes come alive, Venus truant from Olympus, the great American beauty. Besides being beautiful – and positively adorable -- Arlene was smart, too. I mean, not smart like me smart, patted on the head by professors, I mean the top shelf of smart: *recognized-by-employers* smart. Paid smart. Her thoughts could pay rent and buy food. The best kind of smart. My dear Arlene was already under signed contract with a Cambridge think tank, to start this summer, two weeks into August, at six figures. The bonus she would receive would pay for five trips around the world. She was going to have her own office, her own secretary and two researchers.

And here she was, caring for me for nothing. What a lady. Into my hospital room, Arlene brought a heavy, enigmatic bagful of books, which turned out to be a half-shelf of large Nixon biographies, one on Pat and Dick, *Six Crises* and *RN*, Volume One of his memoirs. What she offered me next explained the books: a magazine, folded to a full-page ad.

As I read, I saw that, besides the huge prize offered, the ad's weird sample requirement snagged my riveted attention. Arlene obviously expected this. Probably thinking that it would be decisive, in red ink Arlene had underlined the sample requirement and written large, looping margin comments: *Amazing. A Nixon writing contest!?*

Without hesitation, I told Arlene, "I've got to enter this."

The contest's $ 50,000 prize money, not to mention a year's free residence in luxurious isolation, would buy me just the time I needed to finish the Great American Novel, the one floating downriver in a flatboat with Lincoln, his step-brother, his cousin and the oddball horse-whisperer, Denton Offutt, that I had been scribbling for the last six months of my college education, stealing hours from precious sleep by not hitting the hay until long after midnight. Everything, everything else that I could, I put on hold. It had been classes, work, novel, sleep, classes, work, novel, sleep. Every day the same, Gabe the Unapologetic Novelist with no other life, not even my favorite bowling, beer and cheese crunches with friends. I ignored not only love but the economics of necessity that made the idea of Arlene and me living together compelling. I was intent on making my mark with a book, to reach escape velocity from poverty as a 21-year old holder of a Harvard degree in History whose father was playing Stalin on a bad day. Unless rescued by a job teaching pimpled, gum-chewing, cell phone-fetuses history, I was sure that I was otherwise doomed to doing the Man's bidding at sandwich shops, photocopy centers or ushering at sports events until the day I died on one of those hated jobs and that was no life at all, besides being so poorly compensated.

I thought about the odds here. Almost anyone was eligible, but surely not many would try: *Who else is going to write about Dick Nixon meeting his future wife in a church basement auditioning for some jerk play? I'll have no competition.*

The ad in the writer's magazine, a large grey blob of tiny print like a legal notice -- which gave me the shivers to see, my father being a probate specialist whose life was made completely of the unread columns of legal notices in newspapers -- took up the full page:

THEODOSIA FILBERT MEMORIAL WRITING CONTEST

TOP PRIZE: $ 50,000 and one year's residence at the late Theodosia Filbert's former lodge in Buttermilk, Colorado.

ELIGIBILITY AND REQUIREMENTS: Open to anyone over age eighteen (18) who has not previously published a novel.

PRIZE ELIGIBILITY: Only one prize, the Top Prize noted, will be awarded to the applicant whose entry (within parameters described below, and attested to be original) is judged to be the best among those submitted. This year's panel of three judges includes Rosalee Mercurio, Nancy Foster Diller and Burgess Tyne.

PROCEDURE: Applicants must fill out the online form and submit an e-entry of no more than 5,000 words of a sample chapter (or other fragmentary portion) of a projected novel. All applicants are to write on the same theme, noted below. Entries are to be double-spaced in letters of 12-point Times New Roman or Helvetica typeface.

The putative projected novel is historical fiction in genre, told from any point of view and rendered in any mood, tone or voice. Fictional devices such as flashbacks or future and/or fantasized events are fine, as are literary devices such as onomatopoeia or alliteration.

Research into the actual event, which is permissible, is not required, is in each applicant's discretion and is neither encouraged nor discouraged.

This year's theme is the first meeting between Richard M. "Dick" Nixon and Thelma Patricia "Pat" Ryan. *Amazing. A Nixon writing contest!?*

The following elements of fact may be used or omitted from each applicant's sample chapter or fragments:

The Whittier Community Players are auditioning roles for actors in "Dark Towers" in the basement of the St. Matthias Episcopal Church. "Dark Towers" is a mystery play that was successful on Broadway and had already been turned into a movie starring Edward G. Robinson.

That evening, Dick is the first person to appear at the audition site. Dick, a member of a local respected working-class family, recently graduated by Duke University Law School, is currently living in a room over the garage of a service station once owned and operated by his father but now leased to a neighbor. This garage is across the street from the Nixon grocery store and residence. Dick is newly employed as a lawyer by a local law firm, Tingle and Mewley. The group's director, LaDonna Baldwin, cast Dick earlier in another play.

Pat, a high school teacher reluctant to devote time to yet another activity, was nonetheless persuaded to try out by her friend, Elizabeth Cluett.

Among others cast, Dick and Pat are selected by LaDonna to be in the production.

After the audition ends, Dick offers Pat and Elizabeth Cluett a ride home in his 1935 brown Chevrolet and they accept. At ride's end, dropping Pat off at her home, Dick ends up asking her when she was going to give him a date, to which Pat responds by laughing and shaking her head, adding, "I have no free time." Dick says, "You better say yes because I'm going to marry you some day."

DEADLINE: September 1.

Sliding to the edge of my bed, careful not to unhook myself from the IV bag and tubes that supposedly supported my life, I embraced the real support of my life, Arlene, with both hands and, bringing her close, said, "Arlene, this is just like in that book."

"*Love story* by Segal?"

"No, I'm not a girl and I'm not dying of leukemia. And you're widower Phil's, the baker's, daughter."

"Well, I was until Phil died."

"May he rest in peace. You get one more guess."

"*Daughter of Time* by Jacqueline Tey."

"You are so smart, Arlene. Yes, the guy in the hospital, you bringing in books, and we'll soon be discussing a supposed villain, named after an original English King Richard, trying to sort him out. Isn't that uncanny?"

"Fate," Arlene said, taking out the books and several pages of notes that she'd already made for me in unblotted ink in her crisply-lettered, neat handwriting. "I'll bring your laptop to set up tomorrow and you'll be in business."

"Now you're shifting into the other book."

"What other book?" she asked, adding a saying we had, "I'm all ears."

("I'm all ears" was originally the punchline of a gross joke but we turned it to innocent account. Our other constant sayings were "Laugh and the world laughs with you, cry and the world still laughs," "Love means never having to say anything," to which the other of us sometimes said, "I DIDN'T say anything," in different voices and tones, Donald Duck angry, W.C. Fields drunk, etc. Arlene had stand-alones besides: "Ya think, honey?", "My life, my movie" – this excused any opinion she had about anything -- and "We're a couple of brats," with emphasis on the last word in awe of just how bratty we were.)

"Stieg Larsson's *The Girl with the Dragon Tattoo*," I said to Miss All Ears. "The girl was a computer whiz. Just like you."

Arlene said, "I've got a Harvard degree."

"Almost," I said. "Don't push it."

"My life, my movie."

"Brat," I said, half-stealing her line.

"No, you're the brat."

"No, you."

"We're both a couple of brats," she concluded, stood, climbed up on the bed as the hockey player did with this dying wife in the closing scene of *Love Story*, kissed me hungrily and hugged me violently, after which she climbed down, smoothed her skirt, said, "The End," curtsied, wished me luck and left for the day. A brat but a keeper. Her degree was in Information Technology. Her ability to milk the creamiest, most esoteric data out of computers was phenomenal. She did research so quickly, so efficiently, so accurately that nobody else could touch her. She had flown through Harvard on those skills. At times we bobbled the word love between us like a birdie over the badminton net, back and forth, and neither had ever been more serious about anyone else, but neither of us had popped the question, even jokingly. In my case, my novel was the monster guarding the cave of perpetual domesticity. I don't know what Arlene's excuse was.

CHAPTER FIVE

"I am not a quitter"

"I am not a quitter. And Pat's not a quitter. After all, her name was Patricia Ryan, and she was born on St. Patrick's Day, and you know the Irish never quit."
— (Dick Nixon, "Checkers" speech, 1952)

"How important was Pat to Dick?" Arlene asked, her first question the next day after she had set up my laptop. After asking how important Pat was to Dick, she looked at her nails as she spread her fingers, as if to underline that, on this question, it was all up to me.

"The 'Mona Lisa of American Politics,'" I said. "But I say Pat played a key role in Dick's life. She was at first the stronger of the two. I'd say that when the single most important moment of Dick's career came, there were only two people together in a small room. Guess who."

It did not appear that I was holding Arlene's interest. She was really making me work to earn it, I know now. She maybe thought playing boredom would elicit my best?

"Arlene," I said, kinking my head sharply, my voice likewise.

"I'm all ears, Gabe," Arlene said. "I can inspect my nails and listen at the same time, you know."

"Strong woman," I said, resuming. "Dick was on the ticket as Eisenhower's running mate. This moment I'm talking about -- Dick had just received an important call -- a frightening call -- from Tom Dewey, a big deal in the Republican Party."

"Dewey ran against FDR," Arlene said, showing off.

"And against Truman, the closest race until 1960. What was frightening was that Dewey brought Dick word that Ike's advisors – Dick asked, and he was told, that these advisors would not have asked without Ike's awareness and approval -- wanted him to resign from the ticket."

"But he didn't."

"Of course not. But why not? Listen, this is the story. The press was all over Dick like a cheap suit, giving no quarter, showing no mercy, barking at his heels. They thought they had a scandal, a secret slush fund to cover his expenses. And this was only the Vice Presidency he was going for, remember. Later, the same man resigned from the Presidency itself."

"But where is Pat in this?"

"Hold on, I've got it. This is from *Six Crises*, on the 'Checkers speech,' here's the photocopy of the page. Let me read the part: 'Three minutes before air time' – the bigwigs wanted him to use his speech to resign, remember – 'Ted Rogers knocked on the door of the dressing room.' I should add that nervous Dick only had been given a few hours and no sleep to draft a speech that requires a week. In his hands he held only an outline he'd revised once —"

"He was going on national TV with an outline one step from first draft?"

"From this green outline, waving around notes in his hand like a freshman debater with index cards, with no time to rehearse or memorize, he was going on live TV. Yes. One shot, Arlene, one shot. And the gun in his hand might not even fire."

"Pat was there," Arlene said.

"Understatement of the year. Pat was there just like she had been in 1938 in Whittier, during Act 2 of *The Dark Tower*, soothing Dick's nerves, boosting his confidence before they would burst into Act 3 together and light up the stage."

"Dressing room *déjà vu*," Arlene said.

"Witty," I said.

"Whittier," she said, yet wittier.

"Pretty witty. Now, enough jokes, listen up -- 'Ted Rogers knocked on the door of the dressing room. I turned to Pat and said, 'I just don't think I can go through with this one.' Here, look," I said, passing the photocopy to Arlene. Enough nail-gazing.

"He was ready to cave?" Arlene asked, surprised.

"Then and there. Understandable, perfectly understandable. Remember, Dewey asked him to, all of Ike's advisors wanted him to, presumably Ike wanted him to, and he had no press support. He just wanted Pat's approval to quit, to let him go back home to sunny California. What did she say? Do you see, when he said he didn't think he could do it?"

Arlene read aloud:

"Pat said, 'Of course you can.'"

"All in a stream – no commas in Dick's version – you see? He recalled how she said it to him. Just like in 'The Little Engine that Could,' of course you can, of course you can, of course you can. Pat's the hero of his story, as he told it."

Arlene nodded and read that description.

"Yes, 'with the firmness and confidence in her voice that I so desperately needed.' Then they walked together –"

"*Together,*" I emphasized.

"– to the set."

"Arlene, if you look at old tapes of the 'Checkers speech,' you'll see that Pat is *on the set with him*. And Dick uses her like the American flag in the background, as a prop. He lies and says that she was born on St. Patrick's Day and says she was named Pat, which she wasn't – it's all psychologically crisscrossed."

"Pat wasn't named Pat?"

"She was born on March 16th and she was named Thelma."

"Jeez Louise."

"Anyhow, Dick finds it in himself to make the speech of his life. *Never* more successful. *Never.* It leads to his staying on the ticket, to becoming Vice President, going on to the other crises."

"You're saying that Dick survived because of Pat."

"No, because of the dog, Checkers. Arle. Yes, of course, Pat. I certainly say so. Look, even the next day – this is after the broadcast, before the people wrote in massively supporting him staying on the ticket -- do you know what he did?"

"Resign?" Arlene said, making a fantastic guess.

"Bingo. Without Pat standing right beside him, Dick caved."

"Dick *resigned?*" she asked, her voice shrill now.

"Don't get so excited. Yes, *Dick* resigned. He dictated, read and signed a resignation letter but instead of sending it out Rose Marie Woods gave it to Murray Chotiner, who ripped it to shreds without even telling Dick."

"Lucky Ducky."

"Or lucky Dicky. I should add that during this crisis Pat evolved from discouraging to encouraging Dick to give the Checkers speech."

"How so?"

"First Pat was, like, 'Oh, no. Why do you have to tell everybody how little we have and how much we owe?' Very natural. It was a huge public pulling down of the financial drawers of the Nixon family. On national television. But then, finally, 'You can do this, Dick,' were her last words. You see her strength? As he was falling apart, she was 'Full speed ahead, damn the torpedoes.'"

"So Dick did not resign."

"Only in his own mind. By the time he said, 'Oh, my God, what have I done?' Rose Marie and Chotiner were saying, *don't worry, Dickie, we didn't send it out.* Rose Marie, of course, had a job for life destroying anything that ought not to be kept around."

"I wish that were on tape. It must have sounded comic."

I laughed, thinking how right Arlene was.

"Like an adventure of *I Love Lucy.* Ricky comes running in, 'You mean I didn't resign?' 'You never resigned,' says Lucy. 'I ripped it up.' 'Ohhh, Lucy.' The Cuban music and the maracas. Dick was okay, thanks to a team of, first, Pat, and then Rose Marie and Murray the Ripper. So you can see why I think that Pat was key. The man was at the end of his rope, ready to resign, he really needed Pat to steady him that night, in the dressing room, and even to be at his side practically holding his hand during that speech, making sure he gave it despite a bad outline and did not put his raw notes aside and say, 'Th-th-th-at's all, folks, I quit.'"

"Pat was his rock."

"Exactly. So this meeting with Pat in 1938 was really the first crisis, the must-win one he never wrote about in *Six Crises.*"

I was so pleased. Now Arlene saw it, too.

"Yes, Arlene. Dick and Pat, American history wavering in the balance as he drops Pat off at her bungalow in 1938, asking when she'd go out on a date with him and when Pat shakes her head, saying, 'I'm very busy,' Dick – *the new Dick, Dick since Ola Welch dumped him* – says, 'You shouldn't say that because someday I am going to marry you.' Words on fire that light up the night sky and burn into Pat's memory instantly and forever."

"Wise guy," Arlene said. "Too fresh."

"Fresh? Not the way Dick said it. No, refreshing, shocking, surprising, all of the above. Pat walks in and giddily tells her room-mate – a girl, Arlene -- first thing about this guy she just met. She still doesn't know what just hit her, not really. Overall, a dazzling, impressive performance – this is *after* the audition but still in character – Barry wise-cracking with his Daphne. A great performance without notes by a guy who was never on screen, handing up lines to a gal who had appeared on movie sets in Hollywood and seen and heard the best actors of her time close-up – and impressing her. She finds his voice scrumptious, irresistible."

"She said that? Scrumptious? In his memoirs, Dick said that was a laugh line – 'we all laughed' – Pat, Elizabeth in the middle, and Dick. Then Dick waffled and said it was a sixth sense that prompted him to make 'such an impetuous statement.'"

"That's Dick in his memoirs, for reading which you get an A. But Pat said she loved his voice, it was like no other man's, something like that."

"More specifics on Pat," Arlene requested.

"She's not always clearly talking about that first night or the first date or the long campaign," I said, "but Pat said that she thought Dick was 'insane' (or 'crazy,' or 'nuts,' depending on your source). Wait, let me find one."

I something that Pat told Earl Mazo about that marrying-her line: "I thought he was nuts or something. I guess I just looked at him. I couldn't imagine anyone ever saying anything like that so suddenly. Now that I know Dick much better I can't imagine that he would ever say that, because he is very much the opposite, he's more reserved." I also found Julie's book on her mother (among several now overdue that I had to give Arlene to bring back to the BPL) and I summarized, "Unlike Dick in *RN*, who did say that the three of them in his car laughed, Julie says Dick said this to Pat one-on-one upon leaving the church and there was no laughter, instead Pat gave Dick a sharp look to see if he was joking or serious. Finding him serious, she thought that was *good.*

He passed his first test: don't joke around about marrying Miss Pat Ryan."

I realized there was more to say, and I added it: "Dick did talk a lot, and quickly, later about marriage. Which led Pat to keep avoiding him, ducking him by pretending not to be home, not answering her door, or answering and telling him to go home, and one time hauling a substitute, her room-mate, Margaret O'Grady, to go out with him instead, and, when Pat relented and allowed Dick time, it was only under the strict and explicit condition that he would not speak of loving or of marrying her."

"Wow," Arlene said, no longer inspecting her nails.

"You see, Dick knew he had made immediate headway with that first line. He also knew it was his best line of approach -- but Pat intuited this. Love and marriage became the 800-pound gorilla in the room. Pat did not speak of either and, by her rule, Dick could not," I said.

"It must have changed. He proposed, right?" Arlene said, following closely.

"Rulers live to bend rules. It's their thing. That's why they're called rulers."

"No," Arlene said. "That's lawyers you're thinking of."

"No joke, actually. I know from my father: set a literal condition in front of a lawyer, you'll always coming up short. Macbeth's problem in dealing with the Weird Sisters was that he was not a lawyer. Macbeth took statements at face value. Lawyers and debaters – Dick was both -- see around everything, ten sides to a square. Pat was not a lawyer and had never been a debater."

"Or a ruler. So Pat's goose was cooked. Loopholes," she said, frowning at a long-ago tragedy.

"Loopholes. Dick always devoted himself to finding loopholes. Dick, the old debater and the new lawyer, made his points without having to cross the line literally. He developed a whole new repertoire of eyes, facial expressions and body language that said love without saying a word. And, you know, that new Dick was even more captivating. Pat unwittingly created –"

"A monster," Arlene said, her mouth and her eyes as wide as when we saw *Space Aliens, Sharks, and Snakes on Saucers.*

CHAPTER SIX

Sex and the single Dick

Arlene and I continued our discussion the next day, beginning after our usual five hugging and kissing and wrestling match.

"Were they virgins?" Arlene asked, once she caught her breath.

"Who knows?" I asked in reply rather than tell her how beautiful she was when asking if Dick and Pat were virgins in 1938.

"What do you mean 'who knows'? Are you writing a novel or not?" Arlene asked, her voice rising.

"A novel," I conceded, keeping my tone matter-of-fact. I was having trouble understanding Arlene's seeming urgency.

"Not a history, not a biography, a novel. You're giving people a look behind the scenes, into the minds and feelings of human beings."

"I'd only be guessing. And I'd guess yes, they were both virgins."

"Then say so. And how they feel about being virgins."

"I guess."

"I guess? Ya think, honey? You're an author writing after Freud, right? I mean, you've read Freud?" Arlene asked.

"Everything's sex, yes. Freud. What does Freud have to do with Dick Nixon in 1938? This is a church basement, an audition, not an orgy. In the Sunday School room, Arlene," I said. "You're badgering me. Don't badger me."

"That's where your unconscious comes in. They can be talking about the weather but it isn't the weather. It's sex. It's animal magnetism. It's in hesitations and whispers, hints and winks, a quick upward curve of the lips and movement of the hips. The beast dwells within. They're virgins, sure, but they are in their mid-twenties and frustration city is where they live. And this is 1938 so they know it. They know Freud. They know others are already married. They know others have been pumping and humping."

"Gross. These are nice people."

"They are but they are sexual human beings. They managed so far but isn't Pat attractive? Don't people say that Dick was handsome enough for Hollywood?"

"Yes, true, yes. But this is not a sex story, Arlene," I said, attempting to sound conclusive.

"Then you aren't writing a piece of fiction that will ring true. It will be as hollow as a chocolate bunny."

"Then what do I do? Whittier as Peyton Place? The town was named after John Greenleaf Whittier, the Quaker poet. *The sun rose that brief December day/ All cheerless over hills of gray. Snow-bound.*"

"It's still California, not New Hampshire. Or Clover Corner."

"You're thinking of Grover's Corners and *Our Town*. A different 1938 play."

"They grew up during the Roaring Twenties, flappers, speakeasies, gangsters."

"Yeah, I know, as kids, in grade school. Paper pilgrim hats and eating wax crayons."

"Didn't Pat smoke?"

"Yes."

"Drink?"

"Socially, yes."

"Dance?"

"Yes."

"Slow dances, too, cheek to cheek?"

"Well, I think, sure."

"Kiss boys?"

"I suppose. So she's a smoking, drinking, slow-dancing, kissing woman?" I asked.

"And petting, heavy petting. With the lights out and her eyes closed," Arlene said, closing her eyes, tilting her head back, her arms out for an embrace.

"You're disgusting."

"And you're Richard Nixon, Gabe," Arlene said, coming to attention and pointing her finger at her author friend in his hospital bed. "And I don't mean that as a compliment. Prude. Look, Pat is a warm, loving human being confident, comfortable with her gender and not unwilling to explore the world or reach out to live. Uninhibited."

"Uninhibited? Pat Nixon?"

"Don't think First Lady. Don't think faithful wife and mother of two daughters. That's later, much later. The senior boys of the high school came looking for Pat at her bungalow. They thought she was exciting and potential."

"She turned heads, for sure."

"Pat told Gloria Steinem in 1968 that she 'never had time to dream about being someone else because she had to work.' And yet – not a dreamer, now -- why was she attracted to Dick? She said it was 'because he was going places, he was always doing things.' *Voilà*," Arlene said, certain that I had skipped over the Steinem interview that she had studied most carefully. True, I had missed the Steinem piece. Not that that made me a bad person.

"*Voilà*, what?"

"Dick was Pat's male counterpart with a twist. The big difference was that Dick took the time to dream that Pat denied herself. Don't forget that Pat's degree from USC was in Merchandising, which is the evaluation and selling of goods and services. Dick was a young man with a dream. That captured Pat's heart. It's all in that interview with Steinem, in a few sentences, what attracted her to Dick."

"Dick knew this? He saw her receptivity to his kind of man?" I asked.

"If not that night – he was a good intuitive judge of people, always willing to bet on a hunch that way, to take risks, to gamble – soon, or he'd have just cut line and let go. He dated Ola Welch for years, then dumped her. Right? He went for a time with other girls before he decided nah, not this one. Right? I'm waiting for you to answer."

"You're right, except that Ola dumped Dick," I said. "But go on."

"Pat came through, a loud and clear signal. We ask only how soon, not if Dick was aware that he had a good horse to bet on. How quickly? In the church basement – or before the church basement – he knew to pursue Pat no matter how long, no matter how discouraging, no matter what conditions were imposed or present. Dick knew this at some point and I'd bet sooner rather than later."

Absorbing this all as fast as I could, I finally said, "Regardless of how she described it to Gloria Steinem later, okay, sure, Pat knew it, her attraction to the dreaming he was doing, his ambition, and him being a going-places guy. Moth to a flame, and she was not displeased about the attraction, their growing connection. Never. For all the surface tension, his irritating clinginess, his octopus-like suffocating presence, Pat never refused to go out with handsome Dick Nixon but she absolutely made him promise something."

"She did. A gag rule. Not to say he loved her or talk about marriage," Arlene said, adding, "You see? She wanted fun."

"But good, clean, innocent fun," I said, spoiling it.

"What cave do you live in? Just so I know."

"Some people have morals," I said. "This is before the Sexual Revolution."

"You are so Dick Nixon. And, again, I mean no compliment."

"Oho, you don't know the half of it, Arlene," I said, suddenly thinking of something that convinced me that Arlene might be right, though not about Pat – about Dick. It happened after Dick had his hooks in deep. "He invited Pat away for a weekend of good, clean fun."

"So?"

"So -- only Dick said 'fun,' not 'good' and 'clean.' Pat refused in disgust."

"Now you're cooking, Babe. Pat knew or thought she knew that Dick had something ucky in mind," Arlene said.

"Fun. Like he said. That kind of fun. Just plain, um, fun. Begins with F, second letter U. You know, he almost admitted it. Skimming past confessing, Dick wrote back a new note to Pat saying how Pat was the most moral, best, most saintly woman he ever knew."

"He did. Wow."

"That's documented. The note still exists in Whittier, at the Nixon Library."

"Rest my case," Arlene said.

"What case?" I asked.

"As soon as he could, Nixon-like, not whispering in her ear but on paper, signed, delivered by the United States post office, as if it must be innocent, it was a letter, Tricky Dick prodded a virginal white sheet of paper with his pen to invite Pat to a *rendezvous.*"

"Did I say that?"

"If you don't write it that way, you are missing everything. Read Richardson's epistolary novel, *Clarissa,* and you'll know, Gabe. All about how letters are erotic by themselves, these things men put into envelopes."

"Women, too."

"Arrgh. Anyway, Pat said no and Dick? Dick, all remorse and regret now, quickly washed his Pontius Pilate hands of the very idea and sent another letter how wonderful virginity was and great Pat was to maintain values in a corrupt society."

"Not in those words," I said.

"Try these words: the man was nuts. He wanted to get laid and when Pat said no way, he went into a celebration of values. He still wanted his chance at her cherry. *Clarissa, Clarissa, Clarissa.*"

"Maybe. Anyhow, that was later, Arlene. That night at the auditions—"

"Take my word, that night he wanted to get into her pants, too. Badly. That's the truth. Anything else is bullshit."

"You're a cynic," I said.

"What? Cynic? Look, Dick didn't know her, he couldn't tell what she was intellectually, or if her heart was pure, or she behaved according to high standards. All he saw, all he could have seen was a drop-dead gorgeous redhead with great legs, thin, shorter than he was by half-a-foot, petite, with a face made for Hollywood."

"He saw a *gestalt.* Overall impression, you know," I argued for the guy's criteria. "Don't we all feel what people are under the skin from the way they look, and stand, and speak? Their voice, their expression? Dick took it all into consideration."

"Oh, sure he did, sure. Hey, I researched this, Gabe. Hollywood wanted Pat but Pat didn't want Hollywood after she saw stars repeating the same lines so many times she thought she'd go crazy. She herself was good – after she was an uncredited extra in *The Dancing Pirate* and *Small Town Girl*, she got walk-in parts in two big movies before she quit -- *Becky Sharp* in 1935, her spoken line was edited out, and *The Great Ziegfeld* 1936 – and a producer had talked with Pat about extended speaking roles. She was photogenic, the All-American Girl, sweet-faced, another Mary Pickford."

"So what if she was?" I asked.

"Lust at first sight," she said.

I paused before I responded, taking it all in first. She was a lithe, well-proportioned woman dressed in style, walking that evening into the church basement like Ingrid Bergman walking into Rick's in *Casablanca*.

"Arlene, you got that right. Took me a while but I finally got it, light dawned on Marblehead. What Dick *said* was love at first sight -- he only had the last three words right. Our chat has turned things all around in my head. Thanks."

"Don't thank me, thank Freud. Dick made up words to go with the song but a jungle rhythm pulsed through his loins. Everything after his first sight was Dick trying to make it happen, the consummation devoutly to be wished."

"What a story."

"What a story. Just tell it right," Arlene said.

CHAPTER SEVEN

Gay Amigos

Next day, sex again.

"Was Dick gay?"

"Why would you ask that, Arlene?"

"Bebe Rebozo. Didn't they used to hold hands? At the very least?"

"I can't say there are no witnesses who claim to have seen that, and how they made an inseparable couple and so forth. But I think they were friends and no more than friends," I said, my hand going to my chin nonetheless. *Were they just friends?*

"What about Jung? The animus and the anima in all of us, everybody having a masculine and a feminine side?"

"Like J. Edgar? I don't see Dick as gay or wanting to wear dresses."

"But he wanted to be up on stage."

"Did that make him an exhibitionist? Maybe he dreamed he was in front of a joint session of Congress and the Supreme Court naked or, more likely, in his underwear. But that comes down to the same thing. He was one of us, a human being. And conventional in his interests in sports, in romance, in everything," I said.

"What did he eat before the audition? Something in his office?" Arlene, my inimitable pain in the ass, asked.

"Yeah, cottage cheese and ketchup."

"You're being funny."

"Well, he did scarf that yuck down at the White House between meetings sometimes. But he probably had a sandwich or something light. Even a candy bar. Food was not huge in his life. He'd never watch the food network. Paula Deen would be lost on him," I said.

"Were books and ideas huge in his life?" Arlene asked, just to get me going, I'm sure. She knew that Dick read all the time.

"He was no Adlai Stevenson, he said that. And you know how Kennedy looked so much more the reader and the intellectual. Two or three months after the Inauguration, President Kennedy invited Dick to the White House."

"Did Dick go?" Arlene asked, eyebrows up. She was really surprised.

"He did and he told Kennedy that he was thinking about writing a book. Only Dick said it like a member of King Louis's court. It's in his *Six Crises*, first thing, 'I am considering the possibility of joining the literary ranks of which you yourself are already so distinguished a member.' Kennedy wrote one-and-a-half books."

"A short one as an undergraduate, plus *Profiles in Courage* with Ted Sorensen," my unbeatable researcher said. "So, what did Kennedy say? Tell."

"That he thought every public man should write a book at some time in his life. Like, I don't have time but you do, Dick, and you're a public man, if nothing else, the public knows your name."

Arlene shook her head.

"That was so mean."

"It would have made the rounds in Camelot, people mimicking a pretentious 'I am considering the possibility of joining the literary ranks of which you yourself are already so distinguished a member.' And then, nasalic and all-Boston, 'Every public man should write a book at some time in his life.' Followed by laughter at cocktail parties in Georgetown. And you still didn't hear the worst of it, Arlene," I said. "Kennedy added that it would be good because a book tends to elevate a man in popular esteem to the respected status of an 'intellectual.'"

"Oh, my God. Like, write and they'll think you're an intellectual even though you are not and never will be. The unwashed multitudes will think you are."

"Yes," I agreed. "Like you say, mean. To a man who, if nothing else, had an intellect."

"You remind me – was Whittier all white?" Arlene asked.

"Pretty much. But the Nixon family store also served some Blacks, Mexicans, Asians, Indians and, rich or poor, a customer was a customer. Frank Nixon gave credit to anybody indiscriminately. You only had to be local," I said.

"Not a bigot."

"Dick grew up as a Quaker in a persecuted minority, not that he was bullied in Whittier. But he had to have heard that history and it probably sunk in. Later, he was hard on communists, of course. He did demonize people but not generally on the basis of race."

"Was that political or was he sincere?" Arlene asked. My cross-examiner.

"How am I going to tell you that? Everything was so political and calculated, he might have gotten married for political advantage."

"He certainly picked the right wife."

"That he did. Coincidence or calculation?" I asked her now.

"You tell me," she said, matching my move.

"I know, I know. That's what fiction is for," I said. My job. She was right. "Every time you write, one judgment call after another. Dick had to figure a title for his memoirs and he came up with a lollapalooza."

"RN? How's that so great?" Arlene asked. But I think she knew intuitively that this was great, being unique among Presidential memoirs. Shortest title ever.

"Think of this: RN, in fact, means Registered Nurse. Going by JFK and LBJ, he ought to have been RMN. The last two-letter President was T.R. And Dick skipped the periods, making it the initials he scribbled on papers and letters when he was President."

"I still don't read greatness in the title," Arlene said.

"Genius, multi-level compounded genius, Arlene. Dick first *implicitly* whines – this is between the lines, between two initials -- that the media never gave him RMN, the way they favored JFK and LBJ. At the same time, he gives himself a bully T.R.-like toast that he implies he deserved but never yet enjoyed. Then, I absolutely think this, he asserts his right simply to initial his memoir book as if he were still President initialing papers. 'Here,' he re-enacts for anyone who looks at the cover, 'this is the power I had: two initials and bang, we went to the moon or to China.' Then, last but not least, camouflage."

"Camouflage?" Arlene asked.

"Dick shrinks himself down before your very eyes to almost nothing, no motto, no sense of place – unlike Ike's memoir *Mandate for Change*, or LBJ's *The Vantage Point* – no word, no mention of anything, a mini-tombstone, two letters up with no face showing through."

"I'm not convinced," she said. "But it is a puzzling title, RN. And a puzzling man."

"And just how much can I get into, in my sketch? Like: how much future? How much do I tell about the Nixons' marriage, or the riot in Caracas, or anything else when I'm really only supposedly telling about their meeting in Whittier in 1938?"

"Or about the past, how much backstory, flashback or whatever?" Arlene asked.

"Exactly, Arlene. Except that in this case, everything important is packed into the future. Everything comes later. Their past is nothing. Nothing."

"Well, the rules allow you to research."

"They neither encouraged nor discouraged research. They plainly foresaw the author who would set up everything in here-now, Hemingway-style camera on the scene, just the facts in simple, complete sentences and crisp dialogue. For another type, a researching writer, the rules are vague. What does neither encourage nor discourage mean? It's Nixonesque."

"Hemingway fits, if you like writing that sort of story. The first meeting did have a beginning, a middle and an end right there in Whittier in one night, all of the dramatic unities respected."

"In a short story, sure. But, Arlene, this is supposed to be a 5,000-word excerpt from a projected novel. A chapter in a much longer book that would certainly cover the development of the Nixons as a couple, probably through the Presidency, exile and death at La Casa Pacifica."

"They died at home?"

"Well, in hospitals but you know what I mean," I said. "A story of two vital, vibrant, can-do-anything, all-options-open, skies-the-limit kids going on stage for a lark in their small town to raise some dust with a Broadway play about a Broadway play that includes a drinking, tough-talking broad, sophisticated men and a murder."

"The play within a play within a play angle is nifty," Arlene said.

"Nifty? Is that a 1930s word or later?"

"I'll have to check."

"Yes, do. The etymology of 'nifty.' And Nifty Nixon played the piano on stage finally, after all those years of practice, with Pat beside him, singing 'Stormy Weather.' No, not singing. She refused to sing. She hummed," I said.

"She hummed 'Stormy Weather'?"

"Yes, Pat hummed 'Stormy Weather' as Dick played the piano."

"I wish I'd been there to see and to hear that."

"Don't we all?"

CHAPTER EIGHT

Beginning the Beguine

After reading as much as I could stand of Nixon's memoir, Volume One, I happily idled my time away crafting a rough draft. I knew it would not be that great but I also knew that I had to start writing by writing, and better sooner than later. I was giving no more thought to Lincoln nearing St. Louis. My eyes were on the prize. Callous or not, abandoning the Great Emancipator before he was out of his suspenders and too-short pants, I instead revived dead old HUAC, the House Un-American Activities Committee. HUAC had been the topic of his senior thesis. I could have HUAC of a parallel universe conduct an imaginary hearing, asking one shadowy FBI Agent Nixon how Dick met Pat. It was a literary *hommage* to E.B. White's fabulous story, "Afternoon of an American Boy." E.B. had gone out on a date with the kid sister of J. Parnell Thomas, the Chairman of HUAC one time. He ended poignantly with himself as witness placed uncomfortably back into his earliest days of dating by the Chairman's hammering question:

"Do you recall an afternoon, along about the middle of the second decade of this century, when you took my sister to the Plaza Hotel for tea under the grossly misleading and false pretext that you knew how to dance?"

In tracing back to Dick's first meeting with Pat, I, too, was evoking what E.B. White gloriously captured and characterized as "that precious, brief moment in life before love's pages, through constant reference, had become dog-eared, and before its narrative, through sheer competence, had lost the first, wild sense of derring-do."

It was inspired. First, I wrote on a legal-size yellow pad:

Dear Diary,

In going to the Saint Matthias Church for an audition (I am going to play Daphne, and I do NOT want to sing) I auditioned for WIFE. No doubt the Assistant Principal is behind this. He was very particular about my auditioning for this particular play. He said it was because "all the teachers are going," which was true (four besides Liz and me, including Dot, Meliss, Jane and Ann). Except for Meliss and Ann, we all got parts. But what he said was NOT the real reason. The assistant city lawyer, Dick Nixon, has to have been in on this, too. I am positive that these two men plotted . They want hours and hours of time, rehearsing because – of course – Dick got the only role he would accept -- as MY PLAYBOY ESCORT.

Do you think that I did anything to deserve this?

I have to add that Dick the playboy, who has a button nose and his face is just all teeth when he smiles, asked me when I would go out with him and when I said never (actually, more politely, that I was very busy) he then blurted out a wise-crack I found very unfunny of how was he going to marry me if I wouldn't give him a date.

Men don't know a thing, I looked at him really sharply and just said nothing, like you do to show he was in bad taste. Then, when I was walking into the house, finding my key, he drove off tooting his horn. I would not give him the satisfaction of looking back at him. If I never see him again, it will be too soon but – more's the pity, my Dad would say – I'm stuck rehearsing and in a show with this guy until February 18. I am counting the days. At least, with the other teachers around, I'm not alone with him. He does have a nice voice.

But Pat was not the point of view contest judges craved. I was competing with people using third person and quoting Dick, or even first-person Dick. I put the diary entry aside and tried again, a mixed-chronology alternative history chapter from a novel beginning in a hearing room in Washington in about 1960.

Mr. Nixon was addressed by salt-and-pepper, curly-haired Senator Higgins of New Hampshire, the Committee Chairman. Wearing a suit with a red bow-tie, Higgins resembled a tanned and slim Charles Lindbergh except with a bigger smile as he said:

"The Committee and I thank you for appearing voluntarily, Mr. Nixon. As you may know, it is customary that before we ask questions, should you wish to make a statement first, you may do so uninterrupted. On that point, what is your wish, sir?"

Dick looked around the room, all of its benches filled with whispering gawkers, before taking in the eight faces of Committee members, ending with the Chairman's who, alone among them, smiled.

"Mr. Chairman," Dick said, electing to put his hands on the table around the microphone rather than hold them up in the air trembling. "This is my first instance of speaking publicly outside of court appearance and I don't think anything I can say will satisfy everybody. But I will try and tell my story.

"It will possibly disappoint people in this room that the only reason I became involved in an audition was because there was nothing else doing. I had already seen 'The Searchers' and I usually liked John Wayne, although I didn't get his Genghis Khan in 'The Conqueror.' I guess that the problem there was that he spoke his lines

just like John Wayne and you don't expect Genghis Khan to say 'I sorta kinda figured I oughta reshape somebody's big nose' but that's not what I'm here for today.

Whittier only has one movie-house, you see, and when it extends a movie two or three weeks, many of us look for something else to do. In my case, I was interested in the audition. Thank you, Mr. Chairman."

Higgins, having promised to allow the witness an uninterrupted speaking opportunity and being a man of his word, had permitted rambling. After all, this was not the first time that somebody had given a rambling speech in Congress.

"Do you recall an evening in about late winter or early spring, this past year when you appeared at an audition for 'The Dark Tower' *under the grossly misleading and false pretext that you knew how to act?"*

Dick winced and said in a loud voice, "I can act, Mr. Chairman," just before he was gaveled down.

Reporters in the room, who

I stopped there, put down my pencil and immediately tore it up. Nixon hated the press, too, especially newspaper reporters.

I rustled through photocopies Arlene made. Aha. Eureka. I found something great. My Golden Chalice. The Holy Grail. This was a short love note from Dick to Pat. It contained the immortal words of Dick Nixon, Lover:

"You see I too live in a world of make believe – especially in this love business," I read. What lady would not savor those last three words? His courtship of his bride-to-be was "this love business." He had no clue. Daffy Dick went on, "And sometimes I fear I don't know when I'm serious and when I'm not."

Now, that deserved an award for Most Opaque Declaration of Love Ever. Opening the door to enter the World of Love -- LOVE BUSINESS is the plaque on the door to the cellar -- and only stumbling, falling down the stairs all the way to the basement floor. "Jack and Jill," in three arias:

First: I love you. I love you. I love you.

Then: In this Love Business.

Lastly: Am I serious? I fear I do not know.

Is that not wonderful? I fear that I do not know what wonderful is if that is not wonderful.

Plus spooky, even bizarre. Not that Dick did not *know* if he was serious but, get this precisely: he felt fear – fear *in waves* – fear came and went that he did not know -- and might not, in fact, be -- "serious."

I read it and re-read its lines and could not get over its resonances. His Moebius strip note was just too precious. Almost all anecdotes of Dick in those days are of an earnest boy with no sense of kick-up-his-heels fun. Forever serious. Except one time when he feared he might not be serious – in *love*. Then, neither serious nor not serious, he was fearful -- *sometimes* fearful. *That* is the note he sends to Pat. Nixonian prose just does not get any better than this note. Dick excelled in superficial *faux* revelation, revelations which, upon close examination, vanish into thin air. His trademark was cat-chasing-its-tail logic that erased lines as soon as they were written. Like "Eisenhower was devious in the best sense of that word."

Any wonder that Pat clammed up? Pat told Dick only three (3) – count them, three -- things about her past before they set a date for their wedding: 1) she had had a vegetable stand as a girl; 2) she waited one time in the family buggy for a strawberry ice-cream cone; 3) she and her brothers used to run to see who got to sleep next to their mother and she, being young and small, always lost. Other than these revelations, her past was a closed book. Dick said in his memoirs himself that he was surprised by how little he knew about Pat.

Drowsy but not falling asleep easily, I tried to lure sleep to me by recalling famous lines and imagining Dick and Pat saying them as I sketched scenes of a bad novel:

"Well, prince, so Genoa and Lucca are just family estates of the Buonapartes," Pat said as they came to his car. The sun had set, taking with it the sunlight that had made the shade. Everything now, church, car, lot, Dick and Pat, stood in deep gloom.

"Fine but call me Ishmael," Dick said, gallantly opening the door on the passenger side of his 1935 Chevy.

Pat looked first at her Ishmael, then at his safe and reliable car, finally at her Ishmael again, and then got aboard, saying, "An offer I can't refuse."

Barry Jones, Manhattan bon vivant *and Broadway's hottest new playwright, closed her door snugly but as quietly as he could, got up into the driver's seat next and, after starting the engine, slipping into reverse, backing out, both hands on the wheel, said with a chuckle, "If you really want to hear about it, the first thing you'll want to know is where I was born."*

"That, and your lousy childhood, and how your parents were occupied before they had you and all that David Copperfield crap," Pat said.

"I really don't feel like getting into it," Dick said. "If you want to know the truth."

"I feel the need – the need for speed," Pat said, noting the car was creeping along at twenty miles an hour.

"Today I feel like the luckiest man on the face of the earth," Dick said.

"La-dee-da, la-dee-da, la-la," Pat said.

It was a while before either of them spoke.

Then Dick asked, "Why did God make so many damn fools and Democrats?"

"I want to be alone," Pat said.

Dick was going to say more but Pat said firmly, pointing and yelling, "Don't – stop – don't – stop – don't stop – dontstopdontstopdontstop."

He stopped across from the bowling alley in front of her bungalow. Without waiting, she opened the passenger door, leaped out and clicked her heels.

"There's no place like home," she said, more to herself than to him, her eyes closed.

When she opened her eyes to find him still in his car in front of her, she added, "I'll never sell Tara. Fiddledee!"

Then she turned and walked away. Dick looked lingeringly at his new love in retreat.

"What can you say about a twenty-five-year-old girl who told Hollywood she was sorry?" Dick asked himself. Then, suddenly, he shouted at her receding back, "Someday I'm going to marry you."

"Huh?" Pat said, not turning.

Dick, in the driver's seat, watched Pat unlock, open, enter and close her door before he said:

"I'll be baaaack."

Then he drove off to sleep in his room over the garage, perchance to dream.

CHAPTER NINE

A Quixotic Kiss

Dr. Patel had just left, his usually cheery self. How does one man get all the sunshine and another all the gloom? I thought owls were nocturnal, but maybe not reincarnated owls. I feel like asking the nurse to pull the shades and let down the bed, pulling the sheet up over my head and trying to sleep until my depression is passed. I don't know if I still have a job, any of the three. I don't know how to pay the rent. I don't know if my insurance through Harvard will cover everything and, anyhow, how long it is good. I'm going to have to ask Arlene to be my mother and do everything for me, check my mail, water the plant, if it's still alive. I was in a bad way.

When Arlene came in, I was more than depressed, I was angry and combative.

"Don't you ever get sick?" I asked.

"I don't have time, sugar," she said, smiling. "And neither do you. I brought more books. Did you finish the others?"

Arlene is never sick Arlene is never sick Arlene is never sick

"I read nothing. I have a fever. Dr. Patel said so. 'You have a slight fever, 1-oh-2.' Yeah, slight. Don't feel my forehead, Arlene, you'll burn your hand."

She did. Cool. Refreshing. Oh, baby.

"You're not doing so bad," Arlene said. "And if you can talk, you can read."

"I can't talk, I can only complain. Dr. Patel asked why I was so gloomy. I told him, you break your leg in three places, get a concussion, an infection and a fever and see how bright the world looks to you then. Besides the rent, bills, my job, is my insurance expiring. I mean, when is it expiring? After I expire, I hope. I don't want to leave anything for my father to have to pay."

"Your father keeps calling," Arlene said. "I tell him that you're doing well and that you send your regards."

"You naughty, naughty girl. Two lies."

"I did not say you send kind regards or best wishes. Regard means a look, a glance. You are constantly looking, glancing, thinking, remembering your old man, aren't you? That is true, don't tell me otherwise. And as for you, you are doing well."

She began to climb to be in position to kiss me.

"Don't kiss me, it might be catchy."

"I'm never sick," Arlene said, and kissed me. A cool kiss, a delight, sheer pleasure. A cool breeze in a fever dream. Lips of ecstasy. The day did seem a little brighter all of a sudden.

"Did you ever read *The Moviegoer*?" I asked Arlene

"Yes. Walker Percy. William Holden was the movie star."

"Exactly, to be touched by William Holden was to be 'certified.' If you were certified, you were Somebody and no longer Anybody Anyplace."

"Pat had been in a movie."

"And Dick wanted to be certified. Think Nietzsche."

"Nietzsche? Why?" Arlene asked me.

"'Thus I willed it.' Nietzsche's famous saying. But this willpower has its parallel in the first novel."

"*Don Quixote*."

"Don Quixote and Dulcinea. Don wills Aldonza into Lady Dulcinea. Or take Faust and how Faust fixed his attention upon the maid, Margaret," I said.

"Did Dick read Nietzsche and Goethe?"

"Doesn't matter. Or Shakespeare's plays. Dick had these same thoughts, not uncommon but universal. That's why Nietzsche and Goethe and Shakespeare are popular. They address universal themes," I said.

"Dick was looking for a woman he could think of as Dulcinea?"

"Ideally also to be certified Somebody, by a movie star, in another phrase, by One Who Was Connected. Remember what Pat said she lived for, her greatest pleasure."

"Connecting people to the real world," she said, really getting it. Yes.

"Dick was the Whirling Dervish, all action and up in the air. His boss at the little law firm, Mewley saw this and acted. He gave Dick an office of his own in La Habra, then quickly named Dick a partner, gave him encouragement and time off to make speeches to civic clubs, and boosted him into business with a running start as the president of Citra-Frost. But, Arlene, these all came later. When he met Pat Dick was still at loose ends, a Whirling Dervish, alienated, separate, connected to nobody. He needed some sort of marriage."

"So his remark was profound," she said. My wonder girl.

"Wise, self-knowledge. He was serious. Pat looked at him sharply and *he stared back*, unblinking, dark pools. She marched on right into the house telling her room-mate in wonder first thing that 'this guy had told her he was going to marry her.' Serious news, absolutely no joke."

"Thus I willed it," Arlene said. Right, right, right.

"Thus I willed it. This was the first time of willing for the guy whose parents told him to go to school in Whittier, then

Fullerton, then back to Whittier, to mind the store, to learn to play six instruments, then go to Whittier College, and Duke, where he kept up his flow of letters home to his parents and to Ola. Dick never argued with his father and never had to argue with his mother. Now, in 1937, he swung on his own and what happened? Three strikes, no Ola, no job in New York, no FBI job. He was out. He was in a fugue state, in an existential crisis, driving his brown 1935 Chevy into the parking lot next to the Saint Matthias Church to try out for a play."

"A substitute for pistol and a ball, just like Ishmael," she said, not wrongly. Dick was pretty depressed and may have considered ending it all.

"His answer to Camus, to the perpetual question, to be or not to be," I said.

"To be – in a play," she said.

"To be – married," I said.

Arlene was now ready to summarize.

"So, you're writing *The Adventures of Dick Nixon*, a picaresque *bildungsroman* without a story arc but a series of episodes he keeps running into by chance, characters like LaDonna, Pat, his own role, an *alter ego* as sophisticated playwright Barry Jones, Liz Cluett, and that Italian guy, Luigi's son, his role model in romance."

"Joe," I said.

"Joe, yes. The one who told his girl that they'd get to be a *coppia*, a couple."

"Thus he willed it," I said. "Joe was a natural Nietzsche."

CHAPTER TEN

Throwing Out Lines or, Writing a Novel

Throwing Out Lines or, Writing a Novel

I got another pillow (Arlene plumped it up and fitted it so I'd be seated more vertically) and made myself think of possible first lines, no more, no less. My concentration was good enough for that much. What would make a *great* first line? A first line was the key. Every fish ever hooked was hooked on the first line or not at all. Nobody read past a bad first line. And dictionaries were the treasure-chests that held the words for the first line that would amaze and bring them into my tent. How about first, first?

Richard M. Nixon, later thirty-seventh President of the United States, the first ever to resign from that office, was the first to arrive at the St. Matthias Episcopal Church to try out for a part in "The Dark Tower."

I threw that away.

Next.

Dick looked around, eyeballs right, eyeballs left, in that shifty way of his.

No.

Tear, rip, toss.

Next.

When Pat walked into the basement, she saw faces familiar from previous productions of the Whittier Community Players, plus one stranger.

Almost. Good alliteration. "Faces familiar from." Keep trying, Shakespeare. First person, anyone?

I am not a crook, not yet anyway.

Okay, you've had your laugh, now get off the stage. Tear, rip, toss.

God, she was thin. And beautiful.

Scarlett O'Hara meets Barbara Cartland. Inner male dialogue is interesting but only later, not first line. Too confusing. Besides, there is way too much expectation luggage in following a thin, willowy girl around as this young guy ogles her – expectation of romance he cannot deliver. He wears rubbers and carries an umbrella if there's a cloud in the sky and he'd would wear spats if it were the 1920s, not being a fashion-plate but conventional. Everything he wore could be bought out of a Sears catalog. Nah. Try again.

Sex. That's what the little man with shifty eyes was thinking about. Lots of sex.

In your dreams, Humbert. Tear, rip, toss.

Dick parked the roadster. He and his brother, Donald, did not fight over driving it tonight, Tuesday. Saturdays were something else for the brothers. Even though neither of them had a steady girl-friend, rotating Saturdays was not working very well.

So what? I tore out the page and ripped it into quarters, then deposited the pieces into the wastebasket, thinking: yeah, right, roadster -- the car was a brown 1935 Chevy sedan. It had a Nixonian character as a safe, reliable, thrifty man's car. I really should describe it.

"Park in the shade," Don told his brother. Don was younger but Don was handy. Dick listened. Don had taken over as the store's

butcher after Dick had tried working with meat and only ended up almost chopping off a finger. Dick, bleeding like a pig, had dropped the knife almost on his foot as in a slapstick comedy. Don knew about cars. When Dick had asked him why park in the shade, Don said, "This is southern California. You want the engine running hot? Vapor locked? If it seized up on you, then where would you be, Dick?"

So Dick arrived early and parked the car in the shade of a tall, large-leafed oak. It still looked new, Don washed and waxed it to a fine polish every weekend, bumpers and all.

The Nixon brothers' 6-cylinder, 5-speed manual-shift car had been bought new in Detroit by Don making a special trip with $ 500. The car was $ 475 without knee-action suspension. It would make for a bouncy ride, but it would do and Don didn't have a hundred more for the knee-action suspension series. He was buying a safe, reliable means of transportation with a spare tire. Dick told him when he left – it had to be black or brown so, of course, Don chose brown. Who wanted a black car? A government agent, maybe. The two-door coupe included spiffy chrome-coated wire wheels, the first automatic choke Don ever saw, a happy surprise, as were the two round rear-view mirrors, one on each side, and soft, velvety tan upholstery and interior. It came with a thick pink-covered manual, entitled in big, bold black letters "OWNER'S MANUAL," an item that filled the car's small glove compartment as if it were made for it. Classy. Don got behind the wheel and found that the engine knocked and was noisy, but not so loud you couldn't talk with a person sitting next to you. He rested his arm on a real wooden handle.

Coming home, the car that had seemed so big in Detroit seemed smaller by the mile but, to boys in Whittier, who knew Don and cheered to see him driving the new charger, its wide front fenders, running boards and low-slung long, gleaming radiator grill topped by a winged hood ornament made it look like a Medieval challenger coming onto the tournament field, or maybe an Eskimo bundled up for a hard winter day. In New England, it literally plowed snow, Don was sure. This was the car Dick drove no faster than forty to park in the shade. This was the car in which he would bring Pat home to her bungalow before returning to his own apartment over the garage on the Boulevard.

Finally, the New Bedford whalers' chapel of *Moby Dick* helped my most extended flight:

The strange thing about Dick is that he shook your hand and he looked you in the face but he paid no attention to your handshake or if you made eye contact. He hungered like a zombie, all ears and appetite, for your words. Dick listened. He wanted to hear you. Words, words, words.

There was no one to speak, no one to hear. Dick was the first to arrive at the empty church. He decided first to go up and visit, sit in one of the pews.

There, sitting in a rearward pew, he saw nothing but he heard the rumble-tumble of slow, measured steps as if of someone climbing up in front of the church.

"Pause! Avast!" a Voice rasped, not unlike an old man's, but more penetrating than any voice Dick had ever heard, as if emanating from within and passing through his ears outward.

"Why so fast and yet so deadly slow? Shipmates, heard ye not the story of Jonah?"

While Dick yet possessed the capacity to stand and to flee, he stood and, with legs more than a little shaky, headed out the church-door back to the parking lot, where he noticed LaDonna Baldwin's car rolling up into the parking lot, a 1936 Hupmobile, a two-tone pale yellow-and-dark-gray touring sedan with three doors more than the old maid ever needed. What most caught his eye was not the high-priced car's charging bear hood ornament over the sloped grill, its streamlined design, or its awful headlights, set back way too far, probably ineffective, beside too much chrome, gaudy as could be, what Dick noticed were its white-rim tires, premium Firestones, the best his father used to sell. He should still sell tires. There was lots of money in tires, people didn't buy new cars except Miss Baldwin, but everybody bought tires.

LaDonna edged up next to Dick's car, obviously another shade-seeker. He listened as the engine coughed and died with a shudder. It might do fifty if she pushed it, *he thought,* but it would never run smoothly. *Not that he could fix it or tell what was wrong, he could just hear when something was off. Sometimes, weirdly, he heard something off in his own voice, deep down in his throat, some sort of background humming, almost a squeal. He never could quite pin down what it was and, although he set his mind to modulate more uneventfully, his tense mind-set had no effect on his occasional throaty blurring. Dick, who had walked dink toed in grammar school but cured himself of it, found that his voice was something different.* What was making him hallucinate? *Hearing voices was something new. The Voice in the chapel tonight was something else.* To this Generation no sign shall be given but the Sign of Jonah. Was an Event Imminent?

"Hi," Dick said, waving awkwardly at LaDonna. Ought he leave, go home?

"Good evening, Dick," LaDonna said, not yet moving from the driver's seat. "Good to see you. Do you like my new car?"

"I do," Dick said. Should he flee or stay?

"I'm going to call it," LaDonna said, "Christine."

CHAPTER ELEVEN

She was witty but he was Whittier

Arlene ransacked the Boston Public Library and found books at the library on Nixon, including Nixon in the 1930s. She skimmed them first herself, even making some notes before she brought the books and her helpful notes in to me at the hospital.

"From Boston Public," Arlene said.

"Fred Allen used to work there, a library page before he went into vaudeville. One of America's wickedest wits. Never made the transition from radio to TV, not like Jack Benny. Allen and Benny had a feud going by the time Dick met Pat. The innovative radio show 'Allen's Alley' fathered 'Laugh In' and grandfathered 'Saturday Night Live.' Dick appeared on Laugh In, you know."

"Ah, that's right," Arlene said. "They used to have shows on the radio."

"Right," I said. "No more detours. As Dwight Eisenhower once said, 'Let's clean up the mess in Whittier.'"

"Washington," she said.

"You know what I mean," I said. "I paraphrase. Pair of phrases here, pair of phrases there, pretty soon you're talking novel."

I piled into what she found for me. Although I, in the usual phrase, "knew all about" Nixon, it was really only the later Nixon, the Congressman, the Vice President, the President and the Resignee-in-Exile Nixon that I was most familiar with. By studying the books that Arlene had so carefully selected and brought in, I found much to learn that I had never known about a Nixon I never knew, twenty-something Nixon, the Old Nixon, the one before the New Nixon.

Curiously, not many of the basic facts were actually controversial. In terms of the audition, the first meeting between Dick and Pat, the date, the place, the persons present, the purpose for which they had gathered, everything was R.J. Reynolds cut and dried. The summary in the contest ad itself was fairly thorough. Details were confirmed, overlapping data filled several books. Everybody agreed on the date (Tuesday evening, January 18, 1938) and the place (Saint Mathias Episcopal Church, audition for *The Dark Tower*) that Dick met Pat and that then and there, from which point he began his aggressive pursuit of this reluctant wife. "It took me a long time to love Dick," Pat told one interviewer while Dick wrote that it was simply "love at first sight." All of the authors either quoted those gems or spun out in different words whole paragraphs and pages of the same classic, almost comic, cartoony idea: Boy meets Girl and then chases her.

But, wait. Context. As I went for context, my attention was suddenly arrested. What was this? I was intrigued – no, more, I was blown away by the fact -- that *Dick's father and mother* first met at a Valentine's Day event in Whittier, held at a Quaker meeting house, and that Frank Nixon, Dick's father, inflamed from that point, pursued Hannah Milhous aggressively while she, despite family discouragement of her suitor, who was a loud, brash, outwardly expressive and emotional man, welcomed Frank's attentions herself until he proposed and she accepted. I surmised Frank Nixon's "love at first sight" of a woman who, although not herself elusive or reluctant, was guarded by fiercely protective and anxiously hostile bulldogs, even dragons, also known as her relatives and friends, all of whom made it clear that Frank was looking for *someone he should leave to others more suitable for Hannah.*

Love at first sight, in church, against pressures to back off, are you kidding me? Use it or drop it? Was that even a question? Use it, of course. Let it be prominent and the very first described background, as Dick arrives first at that church basement, wondering if the lightning of "love at first sight" would strike him as well. Pondering yet again – it would not be the first time, more like the thousandth – that Nixon men were fated, forever, generation upon generation, to court women beyond them, elusive, removed, meant for other men -- whom they met in church, if not on Valentine's Day. Did Dick sweat that night? Was Dick a boiling cauldron in a starched white shirt with an open collar and a sweater? Did his father's story really shape his own ambitions? Was the world at large Dick's rival him for the affections of a woman whom he would covet instantly and claim for his own, deliciously over and against opposition – whether her family's, her friends' or even her own – until breaking down, bit by bit, her initial aloofness, her resistance to his unprepossessing self?

You've got to factor in Ola Welch, got to. She broke him in. Dick took on every crisis as "something he would not go through again and would not have traded for anything." (Preface to *Six Crises.*) You can look it up. Let me. I'll find it and quote it exactly. No paraphrasing. As President, he wrote the preface to a new edition of his first book, *Six Crises*. He wrote that each crisis "was a part of my own learning process" with a whole series of "lessons still pertinent." This is in a book about his *crises*, for God's sake. If that does not sound like a pedantic auto-didact lecturing in an emotion-drained, dry way, I do not know what it is. After saying that crisis can be agonizing, he amazes you by adding, "But it is the exquisite agony which a man might not want to experience again – yet would not for the world have missed."

Ola dumped Dick for another man. Here's Dick in that same preface: "Only in losing himself does a man find himself. Only then does he discover all the latent strengths he never knew he had and which otherwise would have remained dormant." The silver lining chaser.

So, what do we have good grounds to imagine for our story? The uncharacteristically extroverted, atypically spontaneous, unprecedentedly ice-skating experimentalist, the awkwardly newly jovial and jokey Dick Nixon sits there. The post-Ola-Crisis Nixon brooding over his lessons. To change, to change, to change. Dick that night in that church basement was, in short, a ticking time bomb of prepared-for-it-now romance, lacking only one thing: an idol? He needed to identify the Woman whom he would marry to the awe and attention of everyone who knew Dick and who knew Pat.

That would be some story, some chapter, some fragment.

CHAPTER TWELVE

The power to question is power enough

NOTES:

Pat, German mother, Irish fthr, christened Thelma Catherine Ryan.

born March 16 // March 17 was St. Patrick's Day// father called her his ST. PATRICK'S DAY BABY, later to her father ((only)) "Babe," OR "Pat."

BUT to mother, brothers, friends >> "Buddy."

her mother died (Pat 14) she bcm homemaker for family. Fthr died (Pat 18.

That day he died >> call her Pat, she said. Fthr buried beside her mother in cemetery in Whittier, ((not far from Dick's brothers, Harold and Arthur, named after English kings)) Irish v. English. Old feud.

Introduced to Dick, not her real name, her father's name for her// Irish blessing.

pallid faces of her charges at Seton. did she should think of them. Dick something said or signaled: danger, stay away. Needy as TB pt. separate from real world.

Dick- don't judge a life by fun; by "is it satisfying? did you accomplish?" happiness in a broad sense// ((This is Aristotle on happiness, *Nicomachean Ethics*))

crybaby took act on tour// from crib to stage, theater, politics

great debater, public speaker – began reciting long memorized poems in grade school

"Dick used his tongue more than his fists" (Don Nixon)

Pat Nixon told Julie>> "He had a wonderful quality in HIS VOICE which I never heard in another man"

Mewley used to say>>> The power to question is power enough

Dick's father's gas station 3 pumps, plus tires & batteries, lucrative in 20s, only gas station on the stretch of road, gold mine

Dick wrote Pat note incl. "But I can honestly say that Patricia is one fine girl, that I like her immensely, and that though she isn't going to give me a chance to propose to her for fear of hurting me! And though she insulted my ego just a bit by not being quite frank at times, I still remember her as combining the best traits of the Irish and the square-heads."

NB- Pat required Dick to swear not to bring up that he loved her or ask to marry her. He found loophole to talk about marrying. love note w/o word "love"// peculiar>> he says how he "still remembers" her// remember? re-member, put members back together; Irish, German; their best traits// Pat implicitly in pieces, up to his touch to bring together again///

Besmitten swain wanted to keep Pat out of LA bus station, off bus to & from LA, not tlkg w/ other men (she was lively, approachable!); drove her himself back and forth, tho she dated others in LA as he waited to take her back to Whittier// insecure insecure insecure but a planner

Daphne is not Barry's love: she is the hard-drinking, tough-talking, bitter jilted girl-friend of the leading man, just passing time with Barry !!! a couple & not a couple// she is in Barry's hands emphatically second-hand

"A man who has never lost himself in a cause bigger than himself has missed one of life's mountaintop experiences. Only in losing himself does he find himself." -Richard M. Nixon, 1969

CHAPTER THIRTEEN

Clipboard Art

I borrowed a hospital clip-board, pen and paper to scribble away, making another sally at the fortress of untold history:

NIXON WRITING CONTEST

Dick was a crybaby. He knew that he had been a loud, memorable crybaby whose cry could be heard out in the field when the tractor was running because his father told him so. Grandma said that, with his lungs, Dick would make a preacher or a teacher someday. He stopped crying and got serious. When his mother taught him to read, he knew that he had found an exit from Yorba Linda besides those trains that wailed, calling him every night. He read forty little books before first grade, many of them with poems that he memorized and recited to himself and then to the family.

It was a past he never thought about. He was not Richard in kindergarten or Dick at Whittier College any more, he was Mr. Nixon, the new partner in Tingle & Mewley. Introduced to clients as such, giving his printed card to everyone he met. He ate other people's pasts now for breakfast but they were breakfasts that did not go down well in every case. Since hearing a particularly candid young beauty's accounts of exploits in the boudoir, during which he had blushed fifteen colors of the rainbow, but did not stop her on grounds of irrelevance, he thought a lot about how differently others were in discussing, describing their pasts in intimate – the very word – detail. Nobody seemed to lie or, if they did, to lie well, to know the little tricks of vocabulary fudging, a tremulo *note or two, or the royal trick of all tricks: omission. Omission and distraction in narration saved his life, literally – saved him from disclosing his past, which stayed behind a prim curtain. Or could curtains be "prim"? He should look that up. Some words will not accept the roles assigned them. Dick was stingy with revelation. The past was not rich and he had no past to speak of, nor much of a family, really, the big memories being of brothers now dead, little Arthur and big Harold, and their ghastly, distressing deaths at home. Some people, and he was one, had to find their comfort in a borrowed past, the nation's own, and move on from that as soon as possible to an imagined future that was debatable and – could Dick debate!*

Now that he was the youngest trustee of Whittier College, they were talking about Dick for president. He would be Whittier's youngest president and one of the youngest college presidents in the United States. He was not sure of the votes yet but it was possible. He decided that taking up a role in local theater would keep him in front of other trustees and their wives in a favorable light. If he drummed up some business for Tingle & Mewley at the same time, so much the better.

Gabe stopped, read what he'd written, said, "Sucks out loud," tore it in half, in quarters, threw it into the wastebasket and tried again.

NIXON WRITING CONTEST 2

What do you wear to auditions? That had been Dick's question last year, when he figured out that it probably was not important to dress up. An audition was not a job interview.

He knew one thing: he would leave his blue suit at home. Tonight Dick was not even going to wear a tie but instead an open-collared white shirt and -- a varsity sweater, a grey-and-black checked one that he thought had impressed more than one girl he'd dated. The sweater was warm but thin, a combination you don't usually find.

Shoes. Polished, no question. Dick wore better shoes now. Once, and not long ago, it had been a struggle and took a long time to get together the cost of a new pair of shoes. How many years had he worn his brother Harold's? He was literally in poor Harold's shoes when word came that Harold was dead. For the first time ever, that day hand-me-downs made him feel strange, wearing them and walking around. Now, bringing home over a hundred dollars a week, Dick had two pairs of "expensive shoes" and kept them well polished, spit shined. No sense taking a chance. In court, you have to look the part, Dick new, the prosperous, the careful, and the up-to-date lawyer.

New shoes mean nothing. Maybe it meant a lot when he could not afford new shoes, or when his whole family wore old shoes, but new shoes really meant nothing.

"OPEN AUDITIONS" the ad had read. The community players. Its director, Louise Baldwin, had cast Dick in one play last year. So he had been on the stage before, not just on school plays. Besides, Louise was unlikely to find anybody more used to public speaking than Dick who, now, was an experienced prosecutor in the police court in his paid extra job as assistant city

attorney. But he had been on the lookout for ways to improve. There were no adult debating clubs. So what better way – and for nothing – to sharpen one's presence before a judge or jury than acting before the public in an amateur play?

Ultimately, dressed in a white shirt, his collar open, grey pants and his oldest pair of black shoes, the comfortable pair he reserved for week-ends, he went alone, showing up early. He parked the brown 1935 Chevy he shared with Donald in the lot beside the St. Matthias Episcopal Church, where the auditions were held in the basement. After shaking hands with Hortense, who said "Good to see you again, Dick," as she passed him a copy of some script pages, Dock took a seat in the back row. He read without much concentration. He was not all butterflies in his stomach. He was going to read some lines from the script in front of Hortense and he would absolutely show that he could speak loudly and was not too nervous. The show they were to perform, "The Dark Tower," *was a mystery that had been popular enough in its Broadway run to be picked up for a movie by Warner Brothers, starring Edward G. Robinson. From having seen it, Dick knew all of the characters and the plot. He recalled the dialogue as a lot of punchy, short lines. He could memorize any part he had to, he was sure. Oh, Dick did not expect to be the heavy, although he might possibly outshine any competitors for the detective, certainly at least for the DA. Dick intended somehow to prod Hortense into remembering, and thinking of him, not as a date from way back but a lawyer familiar with court procedures and even, to an extent lately, police forensics. Of course, that might not even matter to these clowns. Dick had seen plenty of legal gaffes on stage and on screen, and heard them on the radio. How often was the telling evidence of murder inadmissible hearsay?*

How many times did the wife refuse to testify against her husband – when their marriage was bigamous and void? But "Dark Tower," he knew, was a pretty accurate story of detection. Dick, without feeling foolish, could play himself.

Oh-oh, what have we here? Enter love of my life, stage left. She's smiling and talking with a girl who looks familiar. A customer at the store, Elizabeth something. God, she carries herself well for a tall girl, love her grin and twinkling eyes. Red hair, she must be Irish. Svelte as Garbo but obviously a talker, graceful gestures. The star of the show took a front row seat with Elizabeth. She ought to be in pictures. Hope to be in this play now. Elizabeth could introduce Dick to this beauty, they were obviously pals. After that, it would not be hard to find a few minutes to talk and offer a ride home in the Chevy. Then, the weeks of rehearsing and putting on the play should—

Who was clapping?

LaDonna, as director, was just then clapping for attention. Clap-clap-clap. Like an elementary school teacher.

"All right, gather round, take seats, please."

He held a clip-board.

"Tonight is the first cut. Anybody who is picked tonight will audition for final cuts tomorrow night, all right?"

Some nodded but only Dick spoke, answering, "Yes." The redhead turned to look. He smiled at her. Unresponsive, she turned back away from him.

After both of them read and had been selected, as the impromptu gathering was breaking up, see ya later, good to see ya, we'll have to have coffee, my regards to your mother, father, brother, dog--

"I'm Dick Nixon," Dick said, offering his hand.

Pat shook his hand, which seemed to her delicate and puffy. Did he work? Not like she did.

"Patricia Ryan," she said, "but they call me Pat."

"May I call you Pat?"

"Sure," she said.

How many times after that did he ask Pat out before she said yes? They disagreed. He said three times, she said six or seven. The new, pretty teacher of bookkeeping, shorthand and typing at the Whittier Union High School only said yes to meeting Dick at the Kiwanis Young Professionals Club Ladies' Night. That was the night he found out that both his mother and Pat had worked caring for TB patients. He was going to tell his mother that, and get Pat his mother's recipe for boysenberry pie. He drove her home to her rented little one-story bungalow across from the bowling alley. She did not like to bowl, or have time for it, or he was going to ask her to go out bowling. What she liked was skating, both ice-skating and roller-skating. Dick had gone from the world's worst and most inexperienced skater in the year since they met to the world's worst and most experienced skater. She cried one time for him to stop, he was so bloody. She was worried that he would break a bone. He looked like a prize-fighter on the ropes before that night ended (he did sit out to honor her request). He was no fun for her as a fellow skater but he was making his mark: Pat wondered if Dick was insane. He had the answer when she asked. He said that he was just in love. Then she flushed and, in the angriest tone he ever heard from her, Pat told him that if he said one more word about love or marrying she would never go out on another date with him. He promised and, next, took her to a meal at The Grotto for Italian fare despite the garlic. The place had a little band on Thursday nights, an old couple, the woman played a violin, the old man an accordion. Dick thought idly of

Luigi and of Joey. He joked that he couldn't find an Irish restaurant, then Pat joked that they were all bars. They were not getting along so badly, without any of the lovey-dovey or the proposing that Dick really did not miss. He did not feel that he excelled in the role of impassioned lover. He did feel that he was good at working hard to keep his name in play and to be seeing a lot of Pat.

CHAPTER FOURTEEN

The Eagle has landed

"Breakthrough," Arlene said. "The Eagle has landed."

"Who went to the moon?" I asked.

"The Dark Side of the moon, a never-ever interview with somebody who was in the audience at the premiere of *The Dark Tower*."

I said she had to be kidding, she said ix-nay and went into how she found "a bobby-soxer" from the 1930s – I told you she was an ace researcher – by calling the staff at the Nixon Library and networking, e-mailing around until she found Mrs. Frederika Schleiermacher, a 90-year-old widow at a senior retirement village in Arizona, who had all of her faculties, whose granddaughter knew how to so skype and was thrilled to link up her grandmother and a biographer of Pat Nixon.

"I'm a biographer of Pat Nixon?" I asked.

"Don't be fussy. Was Nixon the one who never told a lie?"

"Why Pat? Doesn't Frederika like Dick?"

"Bingo. She doesn't like to be called that, though. Call her Nanny. She hates him. Nanny thinks that he ruined lives."

"Well, a case could be made, Arlene."

"She thought specifically that Dick ruined Pat, and a lot of her friends did, too, who had Pat as a teacher in Whittier."

"She didn't have Pat as a teacher?"

"No. She had Elizabeth Cluett for American History. That's why she went to the show, to see Mrs. Cluett."

"Does she remember anything?"

"You'll find out in five minutes. I've set up a call."

In five minutes, through Arlene and the granddaughter, Katie Cavalliere, I was looking at Nanny and she was looking at me.

"Hello?" she said in a questioning tone. "Am I supposed to talk first?"

"Hello, may I call you Nanny?"

"Call me Nanny, what should I call you? Professor?"

"I'm not a professor but I am researching and writing the story of the Nixons."

"Pat Nixon?"

"Pat's included."

"But is your book favorable to Richard Nixon? That's what I want to know. I wasn't born yesterday," she said, her wrinkled face and sparse grey hair giving evidence that she had not.

"I'm trying to track down the facts of the first time Pat met Dick."

"I can't help you with that," she said, breaking my heart, but then recovering. "I was only at their first performance of *The Dark Tower*. Didn't your girl-friend tell you?"

"She did, Nanny, she did," Arlene said, using third-person, popping up from beside me like Eve out of Adam's rib.

"Is that enough? Is that something you'd want to hear about?" Nanny asked.

I told her yes, but to start with anything she wanted, give her background and, if she didn't mind, I'd be recording her. She said fine.

"I'm Mrs. Frederika Schleiermacher, S-c-h-l-e-i-e-r-m-a-c-h-e-r, of Whittier, California. My husband died in 1984, he was

Hugo Schleiermacher. German ancestry way back. My maiden name was Pingree P-i-n-g-r-e-e, British or Welsh, I believe, but my great-grandfather came out to California as a Forty-Niner. Anyhow, you can call me Nanny. I've earned that on my own by being a grandmother thirteen times over, and recently a great-grandmother. Is that enough background?"

"How old are you?"

"Aren't you inquisitive? And impertinent, to ask a lady's age. I'll only say that I am over ninety. That will have to do."

"Did you know Pat Nixon, Nanny?"

"Not much. I probably know more about her husband, from reading the papers and watching television. I know that he ruined lives and was a very, very wicked man."

"How did you know Pat Nixon, Nanny?"

"Pat was a teacher at my high school, Whittier High. Not my teacher but one of the teachers at my school. I saw her all the time in the hall, and so forth, and she taught some of my friends office skills, typing and stenography. They did stenography in those days, you see. I never went into it. I got married pretty quick after high school, not that I had to but Hugo had a good job and later his own business, which I helped with. We raised flowers and shipped them, wholesale. 'Flowers by S' we called the company, not to have to keep spelling Schleiermacher. That was the best idea I ever had for the business."

"Did you see Pat act in plays?"

"One in particular. It was funny because it was my first date with Hugo. I had just turned sixteen and was allowed to go out on my own without my mother. Hugo was seventeen and already drove a car. He picked me up and drove me back, very respectful. My mother liked Hugo, we all did, really. Everybody liked Hugo. I miss him a great deal."

"What do you remember about the show?"

"Well, it was held at the high school auditorium. I was familiar with that, of course, from assemblies. This night, Hugo and I sat in about the middle of the front row because we were early and had our choice, Hugo was a very punctual man. So I got a good view and heard everything. They didn't do a bad job, you know the play was *The Dark Tower* and it had been on Broadway and everything."

"Do you remember anything specific?"

"I thought there was a little bit of a fight between Pat and Dick when he played the piano, some song, I forget, 'Blue Skies' or something popular at the time – he was a good pianist, I'll give him that, he should have stuck to that – but Pat was shaking her head, humming and not singing. I suppose he was saying something for her to sing. We couldn't hear and Dick was back to us, we could only see the back of his head, curly, black hair. Handsomer than he was later, but we all are when we're young."

"Anything else?"

"Well, yes," she said, getting up to demonstrate, "at the end, the cast came forward, you know, one by one, or two by two, until they had all been applauded and stood in line, held hands and bowed all together. But when Dick came out, he was like the star, although he was never the star, it wasn't a big part, though he was the piano player in that scene."

Nanny got into position.

"This is what he did," she said, holding her hands up and her chin high and moving around at all angles, smiling, "like the star has arrived, you know, the big cheese. Hugo and I laughed over that many times for years, especially after he got famous. Hugo used to do this like a dance, holding up both of his hands and this head motion. It was very funny. He was playing Dick Nixon, the Dick Nixon with a swelled head that we saw that night in *The Dark Tower*."

"Thank you, Nanny," I said and Arlene echoed, also thanking Katie.

"Is that it?" Nanny asked. "What are you going to do with the interview now?"

"I'm going to boil it down for any facts I can use in my writing," I said.

"Well, best you don't ask me anything more about Dick because I'd give you an earful. Not that I knew him, I went out of my way to avoid him. But you could hardly live in Whittier and not go into the Nixon store. The old man, Frank, was an ogre with a capital o, really ornery. 'What do you want?' you know, all snarly like you'd come in to steal a pie. I guess the boys would fight and argue with him but not Dick, or so I heard. His mother was sweet but quiet, you know, soft-spoken. She helped with the store and made good pies."

"What kind?"

"Don't butter me up. I know you're not going to write about Hannah's pies in your book, if it's intelligent. And if it's not intelligent, I don't want to be in it as the girl who remembered Hannah's boysenberry pies. They were good but you had to watch the seeds, crunchy, you know."

Arlene and I both thanked her and Katie again and that was the interview.

"A new view?" Arlene asked.

"I liked that dance," I said.

Arlene did it and we both laughed at her imitation of an old lady's imitation of Dick Nixon's act on a high school stage in Whittier in 1938.

"We should patent it and call it 'The Dicky,'" Arlene said.

CHAPTER FIFTEEN

Of the making of books

"What does it mean to write fiction?" Arlene asked.

"What, historical fiction?" I asked.

"Yes."

"It means using events that really happened to real people as an object of meditation – of what the event meant," I said, although hesitant and wobbly as a kid reciting the newly-learned-not-yet-mastered alphabet.

"Meant? To whom? To them? To you? To the world?" Arlene asked.

"Any or all of those. You are exploring consciousness. That's the glory of a novel."

"Look, Gabe, don't be flip with me, I'm trying to help. Give this your attention. The question is: what did it mean to Dick that he met Pat? And to Pat that she met Dick?"

"It meant the destruction of something, I don't know what," I said, feeling my way. I tried to think. "The literary form is destructive more than it is creative."

"Who are you thinking of? You didn't think of that yourself, did you?"

"Noseguard. Karl Ove Knausgaard. Form über Alles. Remember, we talked about him. 'Writers with strong style often write bad books. Writers with strong themes often write bad books. Themes have to be broken down before literature can be brought into being.'"

"Not only in literature but in life, as I recall."

"And in politics, I see now: the best policy in American politics has always been to be vague about one's own positions but to attack one's adversaries very aggressively. The more destruction, the better."

"But you're writing a novel. What are you destroying?"

"Alienation, separation, man as an island. I just thought of something."

"Go on," Arlene said.

"Pat. She nursed TB patients in New York City."

"I never knew. When?"

"She went East, driving an elderly couple from California to their home in Connecticut. They gave her money for a train ticket home but did she use it right away?"

"No, she went to New York. I knew that, I just didn't know about the TB patients."

"She wanted to see something – and not as a tourist, and not for just a few days."

"So she got a job working with TB patients?"

"Bingo. And living with nuns next to Seton Hospital in the Bronx."

"Aha. Because nobody else wanted to do that job and risk catching TB, even during the Depression."

"Bingo, bingo. The worst of the Depression, 1933. Rock bottom. People were living in the dumps of the City that year. That year Pat found a good job and a cheap, clean bed with the nuns and she also signed up for radiology tech classes at Columbia. A six-month course, she got certified, she transferred to a better-paying job in the x-ray department. Moving on up as the bottom fell out of the economy."

"No wonder she was a Republican. Who needs the New Deal, right?"

"Oddly enough, Dick Nixon. To get through law school at Duke, his scholarship didn't cover lodging and food, so he put in hours at the law school library, thirty-five cents an hour workfare. An FDR program saw him through. Sometimes he had a Milky Way for breakfast but it saw him through."

"What about Pat? How long did she stay in New York?"

"Six months. Long enough to be deeply pleased."

"What do you mean, 'deeply pleased'?"

"Let me find it, I'll quote the exact words. It's in Stephen Ambrose's book. Here, on page 97, this is an exact quote from Pat Nixon in reply to whether she was afraid of catching TB, 'I never had the least fear of that' – I should say that this is from a woman who did not get ill, never ever, she was like immune, she thought she could always rely on her health, always – so it's quite believable that she thought nothing of taking any risks, but then she says, 'And it almost seemed to me they believed—'"

"'They' who?"

"Kids. Her patients were young. As she put it, in two tense phrases, 'eager to live' but *most of them* 'doomed to die young.' Their faces haunted her. She said she never forgot."

"Go on."

"Okay, now comes the best part, 'And it almost seemed to me they believed they might contract health from me...My being with them made them feel less separated from the real world. And that is what gives me the deepest pleasure in the world. Helping someone.'"

"So?"

"You don't see it."

"See what?"

"Ambrose quoted this and made nothing of it either. He didn't see it."

"See *what*?"

"This is the woman who walked into that church basement for an audition. What did she say was her deepest pleasure?"

"Um, helping people."

"No."

"Read it again," she commanded.

"Listen up this time, Arlene. 'My being with them made them feel less separated from the real world. And that is what gives me the deepest pleasure in the world.'"

"Nothing about helping people?"

"Arlene, she added two more words about helping people, probably feeling a need to blur the sharp edges of that intimate revelation. Pat knew exactly what made her tick. What gave her deepest pleasure? She knew. She was born to work with *the lonely people*, to bring into the circle of life anybody who was standing outside of it, anybody *alone*."

"Dick."

"Dick Nixon."

"Yeah. Who wrote the book *Alone in the White House*?"

"Richard Reeves. Brilliant, insightful book. But everybody all of his life talked about Dick Nixon as an introvert, shy, reserved, guarded, lonely, alone, all sorts of synonyms for the target of Pat's help – isolated people, people separated from the real world."

"Her deepest pleasure."

"Who else would say that? Working in a TB ward with dying kids, Arlene. The phrase 'deepest pleasure' under those circumstances."

"Amazing. It is. You are onto something."

"In my novel, this woman who is wired to experience not only joy or even pleasure but intense pleasure –"

"You make it sound orgasmic."

"I didn't say 'deepest pleasure.' Pat Nixon said 'deepest pleasure.' And I don't think she was exaggerating. I think that helping someone truly isolated feel one with the real world again generated those moments of Abraham Maslow, what is it, self-actualization? Help me out, Arlene."

"Peak experiences."

"Brilliant girl. Those peak experiences when she said to herself, exhilarated, exultantly, although in her case privately, 'This is me, this is what I live for.'"

"And in walks Dick Nixon."

"Or sits. Pat was the one walking in. Dick was already there. The teacher who helped get shy students out of their shell – that's documented – encounters this lone man, standing or sitting down, his head down, buried in reading a script, apart from everybody, not interacting, not lively in expressions or body gestures or posture. Of everyone there that night, he reeks of loneliness. Out of everybody, he is the one person present but separated from the real world whom Pat picks up on her radar."

"Or not."

"What do you mean, Arlene?"

"You told me that Pat shunned Dick's advances."

"Yes."

"She did not want to date him for weeks, right?"

"Right."

"And she kept trying to avoid him, right?"

"Yes."

"So your theory is full of water," Arlene said. Of course, the smug dismissal only got me into high gear. I fought back:

"Look, one can flee one's deepest pleasure, especially if it is your deepest pleasure on steroids, a black hole of insatiable, ever-unsatisfied loneliness. You know? That'd be scary, a challenge that would throw you off. But her unconscious needed him – Dick picked that up on his radar. *He* told *her*. He knew that he was going to marry her. He knew that she was unconsciously attracted to isolated loners. The old song, 'Your lips tell me no, no, but there's yes, yes in your eyes.'"

"I don't know."

"I don't know either but I know what Pat said about her six months in New York working at the TB hospital and I believe her. And I think *that* was who she was consistently, including walking into that church that night."

"You'll flashback to the children? And New York? And her feelings of deepest pleasure? In your story, when she spots Dick?"

"I aim to do justice to that night."

"You just might. Don't stop now," Arlene said. Looking into my eyes, she asked, "Do you know what gives me deepest pleasure?"

"No, what?"

"Playing Pat to your Dick," Arlene said, smiling. "Now I want to show you something, something that Dick told a British interviewer and friend of his about what attracted his mother to his father."

"This sounds dangerous."

"It is. If you don't *want* to think a son mirrors his father, this is pure poison. Look."

She gave me a photocopy of a page of Nixon's biography by Aitken. She underlined part of a comment Aitken got out of Nixon about Hannah's motives in marrying Frank:

"She felt he really needed her. I mean, my mother had such a heart and I think she realized that this boy hadn't had a mother and hated his stepmother, and had never really had much of a chance in life – well that was it."

CHAPTER SIXTEEN

Great reckoning in a small room

I discussed what I was thinking from the moment Arlene walked into my room, after she and I had identified that neither of them was in pain and both were well, although I added, "under the circumstances" when I said that I was well. I then went right into what I was thinking:

"In that room that night was one very small person and one very big one."

"And Nixon – RN -- was the small one," Arlene said. "I'm guessing but I'm not. I feel it, the more I read about Pat of her early years."

"Remarkably so, yes, Dick was the small one in the room. The shy, shrunk, hunched-over guy in the corner."

"She was the well-traveled, experienced, well-liked social gadabout."

"Arlene, you've been reading ahead. Pat, you know, never lost any opportunity to travel, to broaden her horizon, to meet new people, to make things happen. Her idea of self-improvement was not years of piano lessons and practice. It was not to lock herself up in a room or a library and read herself to death. Or to memorize. Or anything static."

"Itchy feet. While Dick was 'Old Iron Ass.'"

"At Duke, 'The Iron Butt.' Well done, my love, yes. If Pat stayed home, someone was sick, or the dishes or laundry required her presence. Otherwise, man, she was out of the house at dawn and not back until dark."

"I remember that she did a lot of different jobs," she said. Here my researcher stopped to allow me to give a list.

"Think of a honeybee flitting flower to flower or a frog hopping lily pad to lily pad or something like that, it was part of Pat's nature to be on the move. The drug-store, the bank, the school – as a matron with an apron, her hair bunched under a kerchief – her teen-aged friends teased her, she never forgot – anything for an honest buck in a small town. Step by step, rung by rung, Pat was rising, climbing, turning herself into someone who could someday fly planes or run a college. Amelia Earhart was her hero."

"Until she crashed," Arlene said, knowing about Amelia Earhart, whose memoirs were published under the title AE.

"Disappeared over the Pacific during an around-the-world flight, 1937," I said.

"Anyhow, in 1938 Pat still knew what was in her -- and she wouldn't have wanted to get married."

I agreed.

"To be somebody's wife? In her twenties? Death at an early age. Pat's strategy was to stay on the move."

"To have plenty of dates but no steady boy-friend."

"Bingo. To keep her heart to herself. Arlene, she had a life to live, and a self to make. She was very serious about that. Her outward demeanor was smiling, laughing, and a joyous person to be with, lively, perky. But inside Pat was made of steel."

"Dick was, too."

"More lead than steel. 'The Iron Butt,' remember, who had no life outside of a running-in-place, dogged self-improvement along strictly conventional lines. Academic success, certified, official recognition. He had his eye on being elected to public office and collecting merit badges until he would look like a good, safe nominee to the Republican Party."

"But how does that make him small? His ambitions were large for his situation."

"Small because he was still pacing his cage, living in a room over his father's garage, across the street from the family home and store. His parents could see when he was home, if his car was there or the light was on. Hell, he shared his car with his brother, Don. And clothes. He was an adult but he was still in Whittier, where he had grown up and gone to college, where he knew everyone and everyone knew him."

"It was like he never left home," Arlene said, a tone of wonder in her voice. Wow.

"Even at Duke. His father sent him money, little loans, expecting to be paid back. Dick wrote his girl in Whittier, Ola. In North Carolina, Dick hardly left his shed – that's what he was living in with three others, a shed with no heat or water – except to study and work in the Duke library. He had more of a life in Whittier."

"He sounds like a monk." Double wow now.

"And the monk came back to Whittier and found a job in a Whittier law firm of two partners, one of whom his mother knew. He was as glued to this place as he could be."

"But on the prowl for a wife," Arlene said, thinking: break-through.

But what sort of break-through? I said:

"Sure, in Whittier. He found a woman living in Whittier, who was working as a teacher at the Whittier High School. Do you see any claustrophobia here?"

"The reverse of claustrophobia you mean. Dick's fine in Whittier, it's world enough for him."

"Oh, no. He's a Whittier boy-man, Whittier written all over him, but he hates Whittier."

"What?"

"One of his first love notes to Pat, Dick says that she's an Irish gypsy who 'radiates all that is happy and beautiful.'"

"That doesn't say anything about Whittier."

"You interrupted me. She was the Irish gypsy who electrified what Dick called the 'usually almost stifling air in Whittier.'"

"Oh, okay, yeah, then. Usually almost stifling Whittier air, okay."

"By some weird accident, in Whittier, instead of finding a woman happily teaching in Whittier at the start of an anticipated lifelong career, interested in settling down with a nice Whittier boy, Dick finds Miss World, who has been in movies, who wants to go places and do things. She's only in Whittier on weekdays. Pat *lives* every Friday through Sunday in LA."

"Aha," Arlene said, caught up with the dynamics. "So, instead of thinking of Dick as this third-ranking graduate of Duke and a lawyer with a big future, slumming with the new kid in town, a humble teacher, we should think the reverse."

"Pat filled the room with stars, not Dick. Dick was a dark night – a dark local knight with a k -- who needed someone, something very badly. He was a lonely guy, bitter about it, too, a sense of grievance, neglect, of being underappreciated."

"Some things never change."

"Of course, dark as things were, that night, things got darker. Pat showed no interest in Dick. I don't mean she had no interest, I mean she made her lack of interest clear."

"Rudely?"

"Dick was forward, fresh, really, and she rebuffed him. I think by then Pat was Babe Ruth at the bat for knocking guys' hopes away out of the park on the first pitch. She was good at it. Plenty of practice. She was on the move, remember. She was not in the game to catch a husband. Her goal was to keep single and to keep moving. With flair. Everything she did was with flair."

"She had class."

"She dressed well, she ate daintily, she conversed fluently, she was a good sport and a big help, to use those terms, and she was appreciated. No light under a bushel basket. An outgoing person, a beacon to all nations, but no suitors need apply."

"Attractive but oddly aloof," Arlene said.

"She didn't need a man," I said.

"No more than a fish needs a bicycle," Arlene said. "I see."

"You see, yes, but can I make anyone else see? Can I write up the story of Prince Small Minded and Princess Big Dreams?"

Arlene was curious about the constantly-repeated story that Dick proposed to Pat on their first date.

"Oh, worse than that, Arle," I said. "Within an hour or so of their first meeting."

"No."

"Yes," I said. "Good witnesses. Virginia Shugart, room-mate at Pat's bungalow, said that she came back from the audition saying she met 'this guy tonight who says he is going to marry me.' And Pat told interviewers how she didn't understand the Dick Nixon she came to know ever coming out with that comment. Julie interviewed her mother and got the words as 'You may not believe this but I am going to marry you someday,' although she backed it up to the church itself, not later, when Dick dropped Pat off after giving her a ride home. Julie says it was as they left the church."

"Saying *that* as they went out through *the door of the church*? Yucko, unless you're serious."

"Dick was serious. Julie says, obviously from Pat, that Dick had hardly said a word to her through that evening at the auditions. So Pat looked at him 'sharply' to see if he was teasing or what."

"And it was 'or what.'"

"It was. 'Or what.'"

CHAPTER SEVENTEEN

No business like show business

Arlene was now as torn from normal life as I ever knew her to be, separated from me by a great veil of medical terms and covered by the bell-shaped prognosis of the mortality of patients stricken with leukemia, swathed in sweat of her own feverous making, unconscious much of the time, rigged up and watered and fed by plastic tubes attached to bottles that looked like white cider, with similar bold, black lettering. It was impossible now for her or for anyone who knew her, or loved her, to deny the danger of losing her. I could go to Arlene's side, where I would hold her hand, conduct unreciprocated and occasionally interrupted cheerful conversations at her bedside and directed her way, for that, now, was what being there for Arlene meant.

"She is in crisis mode," Dr. Patel said.

"Crisis is a turning point," I said back, probing for clarification but making a bold possibility clear: she could get better, things could turn out better from this point. Right, doctor? I looked with more fear than I showed him, my doctor and now her doctor.

"Her condition is critical," Dr. Patel said. "You understand?"

"I know you are using English words," I said, before regretting my choice of phrasing as if I were highlighting his foreign origins. "I mean, I follow you except to the point of where you are leading."

God, this was Nixonian. Clear, stridently-delivered, firm-sounding, sometimes bitten-off words and pauses that rolled out as intentional and measured, without being in the end more than the sound and fury rumble of throat-clearing.

"She may face expiration," Dr. Patel said, raising his right hand up to my left shoulder. The man was smaller than I, a thought that struck me with a shock. We were being treated by a smaller human being. I thought of him somehow as bigger. No matter. Did he mean that Arlene was dying?

"She's dying?"

"Not certain, very critical, though. We may hope for the best."

That wording bothered me. I was taking my sense of helpless frustration out on an Indian doctor's grammar choices. We must hope for the best. We should hope for the best. Improper but acceptable as well-intended, we can hope for the best. But we may hope for the best? As if we may hope for anything else? Any other outcome was unacceptable than the best. We were discussing the light of my life, the dancing researcher, the flowers-in-her-hair princess, the cold shower of common sense, reality and ideals twinned up in one incarnate body as only one time in a century, once-in-a-million girl, my girl, my life, my love.

I entered her room dazed.

"Hi, babe," I said. Sitting, I started right in once I had her coldish hand in my hand, pressing and warming it. "Do me a favor and stop being a brat. This isn't your style, lying her passive, out cold and letting everybody else run around and do all the work."

I studied her face, hopeful – I may hope, you see, I have the doctor's permission – hopeful of some expression of recognition or conscious awareness. Nothing doing. No change registered.

How can one person falling ill start you falling into a bottomless chasm, swirling into a black hole outside of time and space, the Midas touch in reverse, turning everything, all your lofty goals, four years' study at Harvard, into the most trivial flea poop? Apparently, we are all born with this switch in our heads, like an innocent little light switch. It's always on, we never notice, we see the world in its light, this light, wherever it comes from. But then someone or something unseen flicks that switch and throws everything into darkness. And this is not your regular black-out from a light turned off, this darkness comes with its own surge of powerlessness and waves, one after another, of depression, followed by despair, followed by another wave of depression, and then overwhelming despair, as you drown in the dark, alone and wondering what happened and if you would ever survive, ever get back to who you once were, standing and seeing as you one time – it seems so far away and long ago – used to stand and see.

I confess a resentment building up inside me that she would "do this to me." That was the saddest thing, in her room, holding her hand, feeling twinges of anger. I was angry that she was sick, so sick. I was angry that she did not get better. I was angry at worrying that she might die. It was all coiling up inside my chest like a great, long snake.

"I wish," I started to say but nothing sensible was coming to mind. What did I wish?

CHAPTER EIGHTEEN

"Dick always planned things out. He didn't do things accidentally."

(Don Nixon)

I opened my eyes after trying to visualize what might have been. I was surprising myself by writing more than a few lines in a day, inserting and then erasing Flaubert's comma, and instead racing along with pages (plural) in a single siting, in a single day. I wrote:

Pat was at first flattered by how Dick listened closely to her. It came to her only very gradually, as she listened to his judgment of others, political figures often, but community and family, friends, too. He talked about what they said, he quoted them and analyzed what they said, both style and content. She concluded that the strange thing about Dick was that he shook your hand and he looked you in the face but he actually paid no attention to your handshake or even if you made eye contact. These were showy distractions, appearances that, he had told her five times if he had told her once, "anyone could learn and achieve with practice." He also believed that the absence of a firm handshake meant nothing by itself, or "could mean too many different things to be a useful indicator of anything." The truth, which was a little scary to her, was that Dick judged you by your words. Dick listened to you and -- he greatly preferred -- he read what you wrote. Words, words, words. These he mulled over, parsed out, compared against other words, and evaluated until he was satisfied that he knew what you were. And he did know what you were, and what he himself was, word-wise, but that was not the real world and that was what scared Pat close to terror in associating with such a man. To no one she had ever met were words more important. Dick was not showy about it, never used big words, talked "plain speech" like a Quaker, yes, yes, no, no, but there was something of an addiction inside of him, hungry for the next words, to give or to receive, the dialogue, the debate, the tussle over how to clothe passing thought, current events and transient mortals.

He captured his interest – not her heart – with a few shocking words.

"You may not believe this," he told her, "but I am going to marry you someday."

This was the seed that could hardly help but sprout inside a self-reliant, casual-dating, extremely busy young woman to whom marriage presented domestic tragedies and who kept the very idea far from her own mind. What was troubling her most she finally put her finger on: his voice. He had a wonderful quality in his voice that she'd never heard in any other man. What was it? Je n'est sai qua. *But 'S wonderful.*

No matter, she did not expect to date Dick.

I stopped writing and mulled over some facts about Pat, who spent every weekend out of town. Each Friday afternoon she was on the bus, the driver actually waited a couple minutes if he did not see the pretty gal get aboard. Whittier had nothing to offer the socially active except that bowling alley across from her bungalow, and that was all kids.

Letter from Dick re: "usually stifling air of Whittier" //

She very quickly decided that to dance, to see a show, to have a choice in movies, to enjoy a meal out on the town, or anything else, she had to go to LA. One time she'd thought about living there. Only this unexpected very well-paid position at the Whittier high school had drawn her away. At or near Hollywood, where Pat could and did make sightings of stars and celebrities, was the glittering world in which she thought she might thrive. Pat's step-sister, Neva, and her husband lived in LA and put her up every weekend, unless she checked into a hotel or stayed over at a girl-friend's.

Of course, Dick would be her *faux* beau on stage for the rehearsals and the performances on February 17 and 18, right up into winter vacation. In one scene, she, as the tempestuous Daphne, would sing "Stormy Weather" as Barry (Dick) played the piano. Pat doubted her ability to trill the tune and she hated to court ridicule. She formed an instant determination to resist all pressures to sing on stage. She would hum, the public and the director be damned.

At Fullerton Junior College Pat joined "The Nightwalkers," a club for girls with Hollywood ambitions. She had been in school plays and was then an extra in movies. The group's racy name was not of Pat's devising and could not reflect upon her wit. The name's sole significance was that, at risk of being known as a "nightwalker," Pat was firmly determined nonetheless to stick around and spend time with actress-wannabes. The likely fact was that Pat, with her experiences on Hollywood sets as an extra, was instantly the group's leader and central figure of adoration and emulation. The other girls' thoughts were obvious: *Pat had been in movies, Pat had seen stars, Pat knew all about Hollywood and movies.* In fan club terms, Pat would never be a bigger frog in a smaller pond than at meetings of the Fullerton Junior College "Nightwalkers."

"These women think they're only in town to teach," Principal Skinner told Tom Garroway, his vice principal.

"Let me talk with them," Tom, whose nickname was the Shark for his snappy, fashionable clothes.

The last of six teachers he spoke with was Pat Ryan.

"Pat, I know you're very busy with classes and night school," the Shark said, smiling, all teeth in view.

Pat wondered what came next and she was not smiling back.

"Thinking it'd be great if you could possibly try out for the Community Players," he said.

"I did before, I was in a play already," she said. The job paid well but the acting she did was on her own time, in the first six months of her arrival.

"It was good for Whittier, and good for the school," the Shark said. "Good will, publicity, you know."

"I'm very busy."

"But, of all of us, you've got the experience. We thought you might become the advisor to the Drama Club but, of course, that would cut into your weekend time. The Community Players shouldn't, they rehearse nights. May I tell Mr. Skinner that you're in? That you'll try out?"

Skinner. The School Board. Attention to her weekends.

"I'll consider," Pat said, thinking that Liz Cluett would give her the best advice. Liz had been the one who advised her to take part before, and would know if she could push the try-outs into next year or not. Liz told Pat, "Do this, then you're set for the year, Pat. All the teachers are being asked to be in this one. I'm going myself."

Dick and Pat's wedding took place on the afternoon of June 21, 1940 at the Riverside Inn Presidential Suite, a large room so called because William McKinley, Teddy Roosevelt, William Howard Taft, and Herbert Hoover had all stayed in this room of the Inn. As spring melted into summer, the wedding party had supper and then, once everybody else departed, the new Mr. and Mrs. Richard Nixon went to another room for their wedding night. As Pat got into her nightie and Dick into his pajamas, on the other side of the globe, June 22 was dawning and Hitler was making the mistake of his life. Love between newlyweds wearing nothing but smiles and war between uniformed, armed and excited armies was made at the same time. The honeymooners woke, showered, dressed and over breakfast learned that Germany had invaded Russia. It surprised Stalin and must have surprised the Nixons, who found together very early that they could not count on the world remaining the same even for a few hours. Clearly, William McKinley, Teddy Roosevelt, William Howard Taft, and Herbert Hoover had lived through quieter days than the Nixons. Dick had to sense more intensely that he was bound by Quaker principles not to shed blood. Pat may have looked at him with anxiety over her man having to do what a man had to do, as Hitler tried to conquer the world.

CHAPTER NINETEEN

Ghosts of Christmases Past

Arlene and I had our biggest, most heated argument over dialogue. It started on the known fact that Pat Nixon told her daughter about "a wonderful quality" in Dick's voice that she had never heard in any other man. When my bird took flight from this fact, I had work hard to get her back down to earth.

"You've got to have them talking in Dick's car on the ride home," she said.

"Very easy for you to say but I have absolutely no idea what they talked about."

"You're a novelist."

"Exactly. Not a psychic."

"Arrrgh, take off your *historian* hat because *that's* what you're wearing, Gabe. *Novelists* don't need documents or witnesses."

"Make things up with absolutely no basis, is that what you think I should do?"

"Gabe, this isn't Lincoln's 'Lost Speech.' You can do this, really. They didn't swap dirty jokes, did they?"

"No. Certainly not."

"No sex talk, no love talk, nothing about how much money they earned or the high price of fur coats, or cars, or best gas mileage. No fashions. But to impress Pat Dick would not clam up either. Get it?"

"Weather," I said.

"Now you're cooking, on a roll, baby. Keep going. Come on, come on."

"How's the family."

"No way," Arlene said after making the Eeeeeh buzzer sound for "wrong answer."

"Why not?"

"Pat was not going to talk about her parents, both dead, and relatives in Los Angeles of no relevance to this guy she just met -- and did not expect or want to see again other than in the play. And Dick was not going to talk about dead brothers or living next to his parents and brothers. So, no family, no Quakerism, no religion, no philosophy. These are two mid-twenties unmarried white professionals on a frolic, light small talk. Current events, California news, bowling."

"Bowling? Did you say bowling?"

"Pat lived across from the Whittier bowling alley, a big local hang-out, especially for kids with cars. You know Dick put a bowling alley in at the White House and bowled."

"Okay. Weather, local events, but lightly, casually, and bowling. Anything else?"

"The obvious. You're missing the obvious."

I thought and then it struck me, yes.

"The play, the playwrights, their roles, the theater, music."

"You think, Gabe? Sure, 'Pat, is this your first role?' 'No, Dick, I was in another play this winter. How about you?' 'Oh, I'm a ham, ever since high school,' la-de-da-de-da. Along those lines. Absolutely. Impossible they'd come out from the church, their scripts in hand, their excitement up by being selected, the group forming that is the cast of any play, connecting, without talking about the play, their roles, other acting they'd done, like this, don't like that, theater in America. Dick could tell about those plays he saw in New York."

"I bet he would. What about Whittier itself?"

"Danger, Dr. Smith, danger. Dangerous for each of them in different ways. Dick would not volunteer sounding like a local, a townie who was never going to escape Whittier. He had to be sick of Whittier by then, having seen something of the country, Duke's campus, the South, New York. He had hoped for an FBI job in Los Angeles or anywhere they wanted to send him but he was treading water in Whittier."

"Why would Pat avoid Whittier?"

"She was a teacher. She auditioned that night to please an assistant superintendent of the high school, who suggested taking part in the play. As in, you like your job? She probably would not want to say one quotable word about Whittier – did you know, she left town every Friday and did not return until late Sunday?"

"I did. Whittier was no place she wanted to live. It was where her job was."

"And would she ever blurt that out to someone who was the assistant city solicitor of Whittier? Another administrator."

"Interesting dynamics," I said, now thinking as a novelist. "It would be difficult not to politely ask the new girl in town how she liked Whittier. And yet that would be a hairy question, fraught with all this tension. For both of them."

"There was also the third person," Arlene reminded me, my well-organized researcher.

"Elizabeth Cluett, literally in the middle. She could not be ignored. But what was she likely to say? She was also a teacher. They might even be tempted to a side conversation about school the next day and so forth. While Dick fussed with gears on his stick-shift, a manual car requiring some attention in whatever turns and traffic they encountered. He was a slow and clumsy driver."

"Nervous?"

"Not nervous, nobody said that. But extremely slow."

"He was going to play a piano but the car had no radio," Arlene said. "Car radios came in much later in Chevys."

I thought about it, and said, "Right, no seat belts, no air conditioning, no radio. Open the windows, nice breeze, homeward bound, almost a family, fellow members of a theater group now. Three adults isolated for the length of this ride, cut off from everything and everybody else. Just them. Self-conscious and gulping if they were silent. He probably talked about Pat singing, maybe a little joking around, asking her to sing. Not that she would."

Arlene got expansive, stretching her own wings, brainstorming for me.

"They weren't going to work, they weren't coming from church. They were almost out on a date, on a spree. Spontaneous, impromptu. The ball was hit, in play, up in the air, in flight, not caught or in the pitcher's hands. Free of anybody's control. Who would speak for the cynical realist? Or for the optimistic idealist? For Dick, questions were second nature, probing. And they were strangers, he could ask away. It was expected that he would. And she'd be batting back his questions like a tennis player. Pat had many close ties outside of Whittier while Dick had none. She'd be protective of getting into those ties."

"But not dishonest."

"No, the art of tactful concealment. An art Dick would have practiced every day and for a living. The art of the factual strip-tease."

"Exciting. All alert, all up for battle. No ordinary car ride. Dick probably proposed stopping for coffee or a scenic side-trip."

"Which Pat would decline."

"Big time, yes. No, thanks, Dick, I have to get up in the morning. I need my sleep. Same and other, this and that, before and after. Things, people, ideas. Dick was looking for a cumulativist. About his age, white, English-speaking, probably California-born or long-term resident, educated, of course, and – in psychological terms – anal-retentive. Not many fill that bill but Pat did. Not on the surface. On the surface in safe surroundings, like on stage with a script, or out on a date skating, she was bubbly, lively, living in the here and now. But her core was cautious about money, employment, duty, punctuality, all that, good grammar, neat appearance. Dick would pick up the vibes: here was another cumulativist, you know?"

"You conclude that neither of them talked politics?" I asked, mulling this over.

"I think chances of that were about zero."

"Ironic," I said. But I had to agree. "Ironic but plausible. They were not coming from or going to a political meeting, no strikes, and no protestors on the streets or any external trigger. The novelist who ran for Governor, Upton Sinclair, did that in 1934, old news. And Dick's ambitions were close to his chest in 1938, he was a fledgling. Pat herself was apolitical. No, politics was no more likely than that awful story that ends, 'But first – foo foo.'"

The setting, I had to get the setting. The roads of Whittier, its houses, the citrus smell, the heat or would there be a breeze, how close to the church was the campus, shouts of scrimmaging jocks, eucalyptus trees, was the church lot dirt or paved. In October, 1929, the stock market crashed when the cornerstone was laid for the new Saint Matthias Episcopal Church. Money or no money, it was built and its organ was installed in 1933, at the bottom-water mark of the Depression. After five years, the economy had improved. Saint Matthias, a block away from Whittier College, was one of the community's centers. The Whittier Community Players had met there and performed on its basement stage when it did not have the high-school auditorium. As much as any place was theater, that place, in 1938, was the St. Matthias Church basement.

"You could have the ghost of Harold, who was great with girls, a lot of fun, kidding, laughing. He danced. He loved to hold them close. And he drove like a demon," Arlene said.

"Or the ghost of little Arthur, who never made it to school, died at five," I said.

"Too sad," Arlene said. "How about the ghost of Dick Nixon coming back to review where he went wrong. Pat is the first person he came close to caring about but – this was the regret -- he did not ask what he could do for Pat, he asked what Pat could do for him."

I nodded, and extended her thoughts.

"He was selfish, he pressured her to love him, and to marry him. It was a cold, calculated campaign without weighing what she needed, the kind of man she'd be right with. This night, this church was the road to Damascus, where he made his turn."

"It looks good, great on the surface, you know, Nixon in love, and this whole thing, a pair of Shakespeare's young lovers on stage. It hardly gets any better. But there is this dark side, underneath," Arlene said. "Sorry, but true, I think."

"Okay, Harold's ghost, Arthur's ghost, Nixon's ghost. Or do that thing that Homer did, having a glimpse of the gods egging the Greeks on or the Trojans, and sometimes taking part in disguise or invisibly, intervening," I summarized.

"Which gods? Venus? Dionysius?" Arlene asked, making it obvious to me immediately that gods would never work.

"Nah, scratch that. Too complicated. But in his mind, Dick can mull over his past girl-friends and dates. Wasn't it just like him to mull over his failures? Sort of *Six Crises* as a romance series?"

"That might be something he would do at home, mulling those mistakes over *and* vowing to do better this time, forcing himself to improve, coming up with the idea of light banter, say, or at least speaking in a casual tone, practicing in front of the mirror, then on the way into church, in the parking lot, 'Hi, I'm Dick Nixon. What's your name?' And smiling a great, big grin."

"Don't be awful," I said. "Besides, equal time, no fair bringing in old girl-friends into Dick's brain, dickbrains, unless I haul up some of Pat's past boy-friends and dates into *her* mind."

"She wasn't Dick Nixon. She wouldn't be thinking back, she lived in the present."

"Why not? What about this one night, she's out with Elizabeth Cluett, a confidante, Pat's an extrovert, and they're both aware they might meet someone. This one night Elizabeth Cluett got her into it, right? 'Pat, you've had so many boy-friends, how many do you remember?' And they're giggling and it's very light, just a game, counting. The double-entendre of naming and counting being funny, Pat has to interject – 'I never even kissed them, Liz. Really. I didn't' – to Elizabeth's laughter."

"Strange. They disappeared," Arlene the researcher said. She was my trusted expert, "Only Dick's non-conquests are remembered and interviewed, none of Pat's. Isn't that interesting?"

"Pat was never President."

"Don't give me that. Bess Truman's pre-marital romantic interests are named, documented and that's before Pat Nixon. To name one woman."

"Well, I'm from Missouri. Show me and I'll tell all about them."

"They disappeared *is* the story, you lunkhead. You give all these names and numbers and a few details, and that's it. You write how they all disappear once she marries Dick."

"They don't disappear after *The Dark Tower*. She keeps dating all sorts of men."

"Yes, she does. But her dates disappear from history except as shadowy, nameless males while Dick's girlfriends are whales stranded on the beaches of California. Somehow work that into your chapter."

"*Stranded whales?*" I asked sarcastically.

"Stranded whales," she said, unflustered.

"Should one of them be a Great White Whale whose initials are M.D.?"

Arlene laughed like the character at the end of *The Treasure of the Sierra Madre.*

CHAPTER TWENTY

Tangled Web-Weaving 101

NOTES:

Pat uncredited extra in *The Dancing Pirate* and *Small Town Girl.*

Dick's grade-school teacher - his mind a kind of a blotter - photographic memory - never forget anything he heard or read.

Whittier college room off the library for debaters' exclusive use// emph. Content over delivery >> prep, rsrch, detailed notes// facts, arguments for both sides on yellow pads used by lawyers in court.

Ola Florence Welch rltnship 1929 to 1935, steady, building up to engagement// hated him until a play, Ola starred as Dido in Latin production of Aeneid (high school). Dick was Aeneas. Top 2 Latin students in class. Aeneas declares his love for Dido in Latin & they kiss before they both throw themselves into funeral pyre. Ola realized he liked her, then that she liked him. Dick wrote love letter, commending her for not being a boy chaser, ending in "love from Dick Nixon."

When elected student president he started dating other girls.

Wrote apologetic letters to Ola, made up and they really got serious

Sister Dorothy read dick's palm, surprised- saw great success ending in disaster. Told Ola, not Dick. Ola ignored warning >>if you stick with him, nasty trbl someday

Dick gave Ola any spare change from dates "for the ring"

Kept up love lttrs from Duke, O. asked him stop, never did up to her wedding

Tobacco road, What Price Glory, Front Page rush tickets, (student rate?)

Dean of Duke LS recommended Dick strongly

Swore in SF Nov. 9, 1937

Daphne and Barry roles; 3 of the play's 4 women were Whittier HS teachers (plus Pat's friend, Eliz. Cluett). 6 male roles, BARRY a small one

Pat never talked about past// Dick never asked // how little he knew about his wife's past, what done, where been, what gone through, tragedy, problems; only the future, what they discussed// up to time of marriage

Pat supposedly learned of Dick's schooling, success, lawyer from cast gossip (not Dick)

Pat sicced Margaret O'grady on him once - dick talked about pat

Jan 16 1940 wrote note/ re: funny guy asking Pat out to a 20-30 (social-pol club) ladies' night "just about two years ago"// "Patricia is one fine girl"

John Ehrlichman: Nixon "a person who genuinely disliked face-to-face controversy. He would find out what the visitors' interests were and get them talking about themselves and size up how to best get along without a clash. He could be pretty much all things to all people, to the extent he could be."

MUSIC>> 1925, took him out of the house literally, he went to live with aunt, learn to play piano without distractions ((aunt said Dick "preferred daydreaming to anything else on earth")) atmosphere of escape IN MUSIC

When won in 1968, went to room alone and played "Victory at Sea" at full volume

In the play, Pat sang "Stormy Weather" as Dick played piano

Dick said Pat had "titian-colored" hair

CHAPTER TWENTY-ONE

Things look up once you reach the bottom

"Gabe, you look really down. What's up, hon? Tell mama," Arlene said.

"Nixon's not small," I said, "he's *lost*."

"Let's talk about it. What do you mean 'lost'?"

I inhaled and exhaled slowly and audibly, one full, round-trip sigh.

"Okay, let's go over his life to age 24. Public education?"

"Through Whittier Union High School, graduated in 1930."

"Excellent. College?"

"Whittier State College, graduated 1934."

"Very good. Post-graduate studies?"

"Duke Law School, graduated third in his class 1937."

"That he did, lass. And took the California bar exam, passing that and becoming a member of the state bar in December. Did I tell you about the first cover-up?"

"No," she said.

"Remind me later. His bar membership card. Anyhow, when Dick was in school, through Duke, you know what kind of student Dick was?"

"The best. Third in his class at Duke. Attentive, studious, asking good questions, giving good answers. Hard working."

"Any activities?" I asked, really putting her to the test.

"Not at Duke, but earlier, at Whittier. Football, as much as he could with his build, Latin club, I think he starred in a play with his girl-friend, Ola," Arlene said, touching upon a most important, incendiary fact.

"He did. Think Napoleon, Arlene."

"Why?"

"Does the name Eugenie Desiree Clary mean anything to you?"

"No, Mr. Know-It-All, but I suppose Eugenie Desiree Clary was Napoleon's Ola Florence Welch."

"She was. Napoleon read a tear-jerker of unrequited love called *The Sorrows of Young Werther.*"

"And then he fell in love himself."

"Not bad for an amateur, Arlene. Yes. He learned love from a book. Napoleon's love story was the triangle Werther, his love Lotte and her fiancé, Albert. Ends in tragedy. Nixon's love story is documented. Dido and Aeneas. Ends in tragedy."

"They both must have been great fantasists."

"Napoleon demonstrated fantasy, spilled over with fantasy, he literally wrote a novel, a melodramatic love story."

"*Napoleon et Eugenie*?"

"Almost. *Clisson et Eugenie.* This was after he proposed and Eugenie rejected him."

"Poor Napoleon."

"Poor Europe. After he put aside his pen, he closed his novel, he buckled his sword, mounted his noble steed and took up conquering seventy million people."

"But Nixon never wrote a novel or conquered the world," she said.

"No, Dick went directly into politics, though. A lot of elections, school offices, presidencies. President of the Student Bar Association or something. Funny thing, it was obvious to Ola that Dick wanted her only as long as he did not hold high office that when he did become the president of their class he shut her off, he spared her no time. His sublimation was that clear," I said.

"Pat falls into a time between presidencies?"

"Between presidencies, a time he was not prominent, active, in the swim, dickering with administrators, and organizing dances."

"Dick was no longer the go-to guy on campus, boring but reliable."

"Boring, yes, but bored, no. Bingo, Arlene."

"That changed?"

"Take the facts. We know he wanted to go to New York, to be an associate at a big law firm. He tried, nobody would hire him. Then, he applied for any FBI agent job in any FBI office, thinking he would at the least move to Los Angeles, if not Alaska or somewhere else."

"The FBI didn't want him," Arlene said with a note of surprise.

"That's a whole other story but for now just let me put it this way: he didn't get hired by the FBI."

"But he did get hired by a law firm, the biggest one in Whittier, offices on the sixth floor of the tallest building in town, the Bank of America building," Arlene said, trotting out a series of accurate-enough facts that were in sum, I thought, ciphers adding up to zero.

"Arlene," I said, personalizing my long argument. "Dick was doing form letters, oil leases and wills. Boilerplate boredom. Dusting off the books in the library and putting them in order. Dick had to invent tasks. He looked around and saw that he had mastered the skills required within six months. He noticed that he was showing up to no clients and no business some days.

Those days, his job was to kill time. His boss, Mewley, liked the kid and wanted to keep him and gave Dick the OK to open a branch office, his very own desk with a window on a side street in La Habra. No clients. Visited by boredom. Dick asked to be promoted to partner. Done. But it meant nothing, no difference in his day. For the first time in his life, Dick Nixon was stumped."

"After all that work, all those years, all that education," she said. She got it.

"And all those presidencies and deals. One rejection down, he was living alone across the street from the home he grew up in."

"Existential crisis?" she asked.

"I don't say that. In fact, 'small' is probably the wrong sum-up word for Dick in January, when he turned 24. 'Lost' may be more apt. From 'lost' to 'lust' in one meeting in the church basement," I said.

"No."

She rebelled against hair-trigger lust, even by the lost, apparently.

"You said lust, not me, last time," I reminded her.

"A gal can change her mind, can't she?" Arlene asked, batting her eyelashes at me mockingly.

"Why, what do you think now?" I asked. "You tell me, Miss Know-It-All."

"Picture this guy up at bat," she said. "He's done well this season but today's game he's swinging and missing a job in New York, a job with the FBI, and the home run he thought he hit turns out to be a single. Mewley sacrifices so Dick can advance to second as partner. But the game looks like it's going to be called due to rain. In 1937 the country slid back into a recession. Early 1938, with crises popping up all around the world, no career looked very realistic."

"So now what? With Dick stranded on second in the rain?"

"In walks Life with a capital L, a radiant, lively, lovely creature, almost another species, sparks coming off at her touch, Pat the teacher, looking fulfilled to overflowing, talking with her friend, connected to real life," she said. "Eugenie la Second Chance."

"He wants what she has," I said.

"Exactly. And it's life, connection. Just like Pat said, Gabe, her deepest pleasure was to take anybody who felt separated and bring them back into the real world, to feel part of it," she said.

"Dick felt out of it, he must have," I said, trying that thought on.

"Are you kidding? Looking for a role in amateur theater? It speaks for itself. There was nothing else to do in Whittier. Dick was never going to win applause again in debates in school. Up through 1936, he was an addict mainlining that powerful sensation of owning a topic and exhibiting mastery in front of a crowd."

"He liked the idea of acting in a play more than—"

"Any other option. What else was there? Go to the movies? Work late on an oil lease? Join his folks for a silent prayer and beef stew? Polish the apples out front for old times' sake? Read the paper alone?"

"Lost and found. So that was what was going on that night. A guy was lost and he found a way out of being lost, a living example of Life."

I stared at Arlene with, I'm sure, a dazed look.

"You agree?" she asked.

"It holds together like a shimmering bubble for a minute anyhow, now in front of us. Fragile, though. Will your vision last long enough for me to write or will it pop? Can I take this into fiction?"

"You can" Arlene said, smiling. "You will. You're Dick Nixon *and* Napoleon the novelist."

"Call me *Clisson*," I said, leading with my chin, a note of melodrama in my low voice.

"*Clisson*," she said, throwing her arms out wide for an embrace. And who was *Clisson* to argue?

CHAPTER TWENTY-TWO

One more time

"It troubled me that Dick told this person he didn't know that he wanted a date, and on their first date he told her he was going to marry her."

"Yes. Not like Dick at all. He was very reserved and cautious, kept his cards close."

"But not for Pat, whom he supposedly did not know."

"You say 'supposedly' as if that might not be true."

"It wasn't true. It most definitely was not true."

"Why do you say that?"

"Whittier was a small town. Population maybe 15,000. Strangers stood out, especially a new teacher, especially a pretty new teacher."

"Pat was popular, too," Gabe said. "So he heard about her?"

"He had an interest in the Whittier Players before that night, didn't he?"

"That's right. He had played a role the year before. They put on six plays a year."

"And did Pat play a role before that night?"

"I don't know. But they were never in the same play before this."

"That was not my question. My question was – did Pat get up on stage in one of these plays, one of the six a year performed in this small Quaker town with no night clubs, no bars, no place to dance?"

"You're saying that Dick saw her in a play?"

"And got her name and, what does a young man do who is interested in details. Was he a good questioner?"

"Great. He wanted to be an FBI agent."

"What happened?"

"That's sort of mysterious. He applied, his file shows an analysis that recommended him. Then nothing."

"No letter of rejection or offer of a job? Or asking him to come in for an interview? Or telling him his application was on hold pending his becoming a member of the bar, sworn in as a California attorney? None of the above."

"Right. The file is just his application and some notes favorable to him."

"Kind of sloppy, wouldn't you say?"

"That the FBI would never reply to an application? Was it complete? Did he have recommendations?"

"Strong ones from his law school and college."

"Third in his class."

"Well, they said there was a budget cut."

"Who said that?"

"J. Edgar Hoover."

"After Dick was President?"

"Vice President. Hoover met Dick at a party and told him how the FBI never got back to him on his application. Hoover called him back and told him that Dick's application had been approved and just before they mailed out the notice, their appropriation for the next year was cut."

"Oho, a likely story. Was there a budget cut?"

"No."

"Was there any notice all set to go out?"

"Not surviving in the file, no."

"Then, may I suggest that Hoover read the file, saw a letter of rejection and shredded it as embarrassing to him, to the FBI and to the Vice President?"

"But there is no letter of rejection."

"There is no letter at all. Isn't my explanation of a missing, shredded letter more logical than the FBI dropping the ball on an application? Not dictating a new letter to applicants affected that 'due to fiscal issues' or 'unexpected difficulties,' or any other twaddle? To encourage them to apply again? But, that's right -- there was no budget cut."

"Wait, wait. Let's stop. Your point was something about Pat. Let's stay focused."

"Dick the detective wannabe investigated Pat whom he was dazzled by when he took his date out to live local theater instead of the movies so he avoided having to pay for popcorn."

"Well, it's not impossible."

"What could he have found out? If he asked somebody from Artesia? Ten miles away, wasn't that where Pat was from?"

"Yes. They would have spoken highly of her, of how ten years before her father died of TB and Pat took care of him at home in his dying days. And how she cooked, and sewed and did the laundry for her brothers and herself, while doing two or three other jobs outside the house and finishing high school. And, I suppose, they might know to tell him that Pat took care of TB patients in New York and was an x-ray technician."

"Did anybody in Dick's family die of TB? And his mother nursed them?"

"You're saying that Pat was like Dick's mother."

"Only beautiful and sexy and not shy on stage in public. What more could a politician want in a wife? And she was Irish and local."

"Dick was not a politician in 1938."

"He ran for every office open to him in any election from the time he was twelve."

"School elections."

"And his ambition was to be a politician. He told lots of people before 1938."

"Okay, so he knew he wanted to go into politics in 1938."

"And he knew that his wife, any wife of Dick Nixon's, would have to be interested in travel and public life and not be shy but have a stage presence and good looks."

"You think he knew all this before January 18?"

"I think he only was there waiting in that church until Pat showed up. If she did not, he was going home and coming back for the next audition. One audition or another, he was sure that Pat would come in through that door and she'd be picked and he'd be picked and with weeks of rehearsals and giving her rides home and the performances, he and she would have plenty of time even before he asked her out on a date."

"It was a Pat trap."

"He was hunting a wife, this woman whom he knew all about. More than the FBI knew about him," I said, having held back the best until last. I picked up a photocopy to read to her. "Although in his memoirs he said he thought he knew everyone in Whittier and, lo, and behold at this audition, et cetera, get a load of this: in 1959 he told his biographer, Bela Kornitzer, 'A friend told me about a beautiful new teacher who was trying out for a part at the little theater. It was suggested that I go down and take a look.'"

"Oh, my."

"Oh, my, yes. Who knew that Pat was going to try out?"

"She said that the assistant superintendent told her to go."

"Yes. It was a set up. A guy playing secret match-maker behind the scenes of this play, a play outside the play. Getting Dick 'to take a look.' Imagine. He was auditioning Pat, looking at her."

"He actually said in his memoirs that he could not take his eyes off her all evening."

"And Julie says Pat said he hardly said one word to her, but then talked about marrying her."

"Looking over a starlet, which she was, Hollywood eye candy, she'd passed her screen tests, she'd had speaking parts, one-line entrances but she was considered ready for feature roles, he saw what Hollywood saw. But not classic love at first sight. Not serendipity."

"No, more of a military operation with a map and a rendezvous time. Set your watches."

"You remind me that he gave her a gift, a clock."

"He did. The best she could do with it was to send him a gooey note that she was giving it a name, 'Sir Ric,' and it had a nice face and she liked it."

"This was at a time he was under orders not to bring up love or marriage."

"Exactly. So he sent her a clock, like saying: *time is on my side.* Which it was."

"The only question is what did Dick know and when did he know it."

"A lot, I bet."

"It makes sense. Was Dick really ignorant of Pat after six months in Whittier? This was Pat, a pretty woman whose social life was an intriguing mystery to the senior high-school boys, who posted a watch on her bungalow from the bowling alley. This was a woman who went somewhere out of town every weekend. This was a woman who had been in movies in Hollywood."

"Lust at first sight."

"Why not admit it?"

CHAPTER TWENTY-THREE

Dollars to donuts

If you had been standing at the edge of the Whittier College campus beside the parking lot of the Saint Matthias Episcopal Church shortly before dusk on the evening of May 12, 1938, you would have seen a brown 1935 Chevrolet roadster occupied by a lone driver approach at moderate speed and then turn into the lot and park squarely, albeit after two needed back and forth attempts. Upon exiting, the thick dark brown or black hair of the driver would register in contrast to the white shirt he wore, a starchy, neat shirt, properly buttoned, and a black-and-grey-checked sweater worn unbuttoned. His pants were pressed and his shoes were shiny black. There was no reason not to expect that he was not present to attend a meeting or social gathering at the church. This expectation only gained momentum as the young man headed with stiff, unbending steps of seeming confidence directly to the side entrance to the church basement. His roadster was only the second vehicle in the lot.

Dick was all dressed up with nowhere to go, as they say, nowhere but church, and for an audition in local theater. It was the worst-kept secret in Whittier that plays were mixers for its old maid school-teachers. School administrators spoke with all eligible misses under forty to be sure and go to the try-outs. In lieu of a wife auction, the educated gals of town were going to be up on the stage in the high-school assembly room prancing and speaking, ostensibly putting on a play, but at the same time in real life auditioning for permanent roles in some bachelor's life. Although Dick did not know the exact number, he knew the general idea well enough to bet on its happening. It would, too. LaDonna would pick four unmarried Whittier teachers for female roles tonight.

What would work for old maids could work for lawyers. A light bulb went on among the small group of men who practiced law in town that they could use plays to drum up business. Dick was reminded that lawyers could not advertise and, as a young lawyer who wanted people to remember his name, he should go on stage.

He'd been on the fence about doing so until that afternoon. The fact was, Dick relied on letters to certify people's interest in him: so many letters, so many votes of approval. December had been his best month in 1937, netting over a hundred notes, some scribbled on Christmas cards, of course, and a few of them catch-up long letters of news from classmates at Duke now getting their first jobs, or at least sworn into the bar. But he'd even received a note from Ola and her new husband, hoping he was well, saying they'd heard he was a "legal beagle." However, January, even including birthday cards – local-made commercial cards, for God's sake – had not exceeded a dozen. Nobody cared enough to send anything, let alone the very best. Dick felt like he was someone who was on Christmas card lists. Period.

That afternoon, still in his new office in La Hambra, Dick had toyed with typing a letter on his official stationery to an old room-mate from Duke days, one he had not heard from after their graduation:

Dear Tim,
How's everything going for you in Montana?
I'm back in Whittier myself

Dick then pulled the paper out of the typewriter and ripped it to shreds. Tim could write him, he had his address. It had not changed.

Between the car and the church, despite blue skies, no matter that it was not windy, that no dark clouds were gathering overhead, that no storm was coming on and that he was not out on the moors, Dick was gloomy in the gloaming of Whittier. Warmth and eucalyptus aside, Dick could use the sanctuary *right now* that human contact, bright light and the exotic scent of candles and kid-sweat of the Sunday school room could provide him.

Inside the church, in its basement, in a blaze, having turned on all of its available lights, stood the hopeful director of the local community theater group, LaDonna Baldwin, who greeted Dick even as she thought it was ominous that he was the first to arrive. Almost anyone was more relaxed on stage and lively off stage than Dick Nixon, whose tendency to freeze-pose and clutch in his first time on stage was obvious to LaDonna's trained eye, although over the head of most of a Whittier audience, thank God.

Dick was nonetheless a dedicated crowd-pleaser, quite attentive to the fact that he had an audience -- too attentive. What was it about him? Trying to puzzle this out for her own satisfaction, LaDonna tended to metaphors, stumbling metaphors. Mute silvery fish jumped up, thrashing within her splashy mind, flecks dripping with *Dick walks funny, Dick smiles like a second-rate burglar caught coming out of church with a chalice, Dick's eyes were deep brown and girlish as Mary Pickford's, prison guard eyes, cop eyes, looking-for-the-bad-guys eyes.* Some thought that LaDonna was ditsy and giddy, which by no means was uncommon in theater production and did not exclude her from the field, but that impression actually came out from a thought flow that was far faster than her verbal stream.

"Would I do for the part of Barry Jones?" Dick asked, shaking hands, his beady eyes both boring into her, almost overwhelming her. He had seen the movie, he had his eyes on a small part with a lot of posing on stage. She had cast him as a lawyer last time, in which he had been competent enough, playing himself. LaDonna had even called to invite Dick to try out that time. For that play, LaDonna had asked those who came to recite anything they had memorized, even if it was only the words to Happy Birthday. Dick won cheers with something from a booth he once ran at some kind of carnival, Dick's Wheel of Fortune during Frontier Days, "Step right up and try your luck, only a quarter, two-bits, twenty-five of those little pennies you saved up all winter to buy this excitement." It had life to it, more life than Dick ever actually showed on stage in the play, playing himself.

"You sound like a contender to me," LaDonna said, giggling less out of ahhh good than to cover up the absence of any sense of relief. "Barry's first line is something obsequious about how he one pleases Miss Temple. Here, look."

LaDonna gave him a script, dealing off the bottom of the pile she held up to her chest and feeling funny about that. He went inside the room and took a position familiar to him at home and in the office and all through school and his life: reader. If you took all the miles of text Dick's eyes had passed over, you could have gone around the world twenty-five, count them, ladies and gentlemen, twenty-five times. Nobody his age in Whittier had read so much, and he was closing in on the best-read of all ages at all times. He lived in books, he could live in this script, and he could inhabit a role. How peculiar it might seem to another passing resident of Quakerville, this California Gopher Prairie, that a grown-up might frolic and gambol as if he were a Broadway cad in spats and cravat, in public but to Dick this was nothing he had not done all of his life, in public or in private, fantasizing, entering a text imaginatively, doing mental hand-springs and contortions of which his Dad was incapable and blissfully unaware. For Dick the D'Artagnon of Wilshire Boulevard and Lafferty Road, being a big-hit Broadway Beau Brummel was duck soup.

It was piano notes he heard, pounding in his head, as he read. *Do, do, do, what you done, done, done* Gershwin, a tune he picked out and practiced and practiced when it was new, filling his aunt's home with the music of Manhattan, rolling out revelry, if only for himself, age eleven, and now those tinkling keys revived in his mind as he imagined the background music to Barry Jones, strutting in with a svelte blonde on his arm, maybe two. Ah, he would play the piano. *Stormy Weather*. That he could do, and stop the show, with the right broad singing loud enough. And *Long, Long Trail Awinding.* Sentimental, a war-time moody sad one, played slow it would move them. At his fingertips a whole other world stood, untapped by the piano-player in him. He loved the potential of a piano, a sound that required him for it to come out, only he could milk harmonious notes out in proper out, *Do, do, do.* He was a bit shy speaking lines – this would never change, he was sure, he could be President of the United States clothed in enormous power, the Commander in Chief bringing news of triumph in war, and he was sure of a little looseness of his grip, tentativeness, in one word: shyness. But give him a keyboard, place him at a piano, and he had no palpitations or flutters, he was a master at home before the family hearth patting his dog's head. He was the king of the stage in this scene playing the piano, he was sure of shining. Only he must not be paired with some broad who could not sing, who would spoil everything if she could not reach the sultry essence of *Stormy Weather*, and bellow the beautiful out of that ironic, twisty, teasey tune of the damsel in distress who sees silver linings in stormy weather itself, who can *try again and sigh again and fly again together.* Just like that *arpeggio* in *Do, do, do.*Would the audience appreciate it? They would. No critic attending for their *Bingville Bugle* could say why or articulate the word *arpeggio* but they would be uplifted and their hands would speak in joyful applause. Dick would play Barry Jones – and, he would play the piano, too.

CHAPTER TWENTY-FOUR

The poor bastard

> *"Last Christmas I went looking for him in his rooms over the garage. He wasn't there but on his bed lay a well-thumbed volume put out by the Rosicrucians called* How to Harness Your Secret Powers. *The poor bastard."*
>
> - Walker Percy, *The Moviegoer* (1960)

NOTES:

Patton, movie 1970, George C. Scott.

Nixon saw it (Apr. 1?), 1970 (Apr. 4?) conflict in sources, spec.

his favorite film

saw it on Pres. Yacht & other times before invad. Cambodia

Woodward & Bernstein = his favorite film

Sectry/State Rogers> Nixon "walking ad" for *Patton*

Nixon told staffers see this movie *Patton* "go and see Patton"

Ike's favorite > *Angels in the Outfield* 1951

sentimental piece, baseball, invisible angels help Pittsburgh Pirates, noticed by orphan girl// The Other World helps us

Ike saw it over 30 times, had it played in Gettysburg farm, "wonderful show"

CHAPTER TWENTY-FIVE

You don't have to go home but you can't stay here

I was okay to go, discharged by Dr. Patel. My nurse of the day spoke words of benediction over me fast like a priest murmuring memorized prayers, words almost worn thin of any meaning. I did catch whiffs of advice, "aspirin if you need pain relief," and to watch for "any sharp pains or sores that are like boils, with pus" and so on and so forth. *Let me out of here*, I screamed inside until I was wheeled – yes, wheeled, in a genuine wheelchair, "for legal reasons," -- to the front lobby. There I was allowed to appear to the mystified but mute people waiting in that waiting area as I "arose and walked," healed, cured by the miracle of modern medicine.

Arlene snuggling me close, we went, arm in arm out of the hospital, over the river and through the Square to Bartlett's Burger Cott, where we ordered two cheeseburgers, fries and shakes. She finished with cheesecake, I with apple pie a la mode. Rich Girl paid.

"Thanks," I said. "I pay the next time."

It came to me only later that she was arm-in-arm and close to make sure I did not fall. I had been thinking how frisky and physical she was. After such a long time. Upon our entry into my apartment after a taxi ride, we threw caution to the wind. Which pleased me no end.

"Well," I said, having discharged my duty, as they say.

"Yes," Arlene said, "well done."

"Spiro Agnew," I said.

"Explain," my endlessly patient Arlene said.

"Gladly. In 1968 the Republicans ran polls of dream tickets, Nixon-Rockefeller, Nixon-Goldwater, all of the combinations. And you know what they found?"

"They found that Nixon ran better alone than with any of them."

"You cheated. You researched this."

"I'm a researcher. It's what I do, honey-chile."

"So they found the most obscure possible running mate, somebody who was not a household name."

"Spiro Agnew, he said so himself: 'I am not a household name.'"

"So, imagine Pat, in town since September, a pretty woman, the new teacher at the high school, but so not part of Whittier that she might as well be wearing sunglasses and camouflage."

"The woman nobody knew, the original Spiro Agnew."

"Why not? Dick's mother was his father's shadow. Nobody will ever write a book about her, he said, do you remember?"

"Out of the blue, the day he resigned."

"Yes. Dick was conscious: no book for his mother. She was part of nobody's bigger story but her family's. For her husband and sons she was a shadow, a constant flat note in the background. Never anything more, no hugs and kisses, no hovering, the opposite of overanxious, overwhelming parents."

"Dick wanted an aloof chick? Not a kissy-huggy woman?"

"Not consciously, Arlene, but wasn't it great that he found a woman cool to him, aloof, holding him off, down boy? A perfect stranger in all senses, perfect in figure, in face, in her titian-tinted hair, and in her obscurity as a teacher who only came out on weekdays in Whittier. In Whittier, she only went to work, went home and went to sleep."

"Dick Nixon's perfect mate was his mother or Spiro Agnew."

We both laughed but I didn't know why. Probably, it was the laugh of recognition for the way things are. I really do find reality funny, how space is infinite – get your mind around the concept of light reaching us today that started out when dinosaurs roamed an unpeopled planet – and evolution, think of how our arms evolved from fish-fins and lower mammals' paws. Do you know that you're stardust animated and modified algae on legs? You can't make it up. Dick's perfect woman was Frankenstein and poor Pat served his need for *La Stranger* in a skirt who would only do it for hygienic purposes and reproduction. Not like Arlene, my very own recreational sex buddy and closest friend on earth, which, by the way, is a dust-ball hanging over from the Big Bang. Thanks."

"Thank *you* for the big bang," she said.

"I mean, for coming today."

"So do I, sugar-plum."

"You're daffy," I said.

"Turkish taffy," she said.

"*David and Lisa*. But you can touch me."

"Are you going to write today? Your Nixon book?" she asked.

I looked at her.

"How else am I going to earn fifty-thousand-dollars without leaving my room?"

"Good," Arlene said. "Then I should leave you be. You, Dick and Pat."

"And Spiro Agnew, a real *ménage a trois*," I said, smiling as we kissed and hugged. "See you later."

"Alligator," she said.

I wish now that I'd argued. At the moment I thought Arlene was right. It hurts now that I did not argue for her to stay because, dear reader, Arlene knew what I did not know in my animated stardust, dolphin-fin-armed stud self; that was, she had terminal cancer. And didn't tell me. The Nixon book, you know. Do not disturb the genius.

CHAPTER TWENTY-SIX

Once more into the breach

As Dick drove over to St. Matthias Church, the road got him into a mood. This was the same road from years back, back when Dick had had to get up early to hop up into the driver's seat of the family truck and head down to Los Angeles.

The low notes of a cello woke Dick, but there was no cello. He was dreaming. The alarm clock was ringing. He reached out and shut it off before Donald could complain. Donald, one year younger and too young to drive, could sleep while Dick got up and drove to Los Angeles for produce for the Nixon store. The cello was Luigi's music in the air. Luigi, who sold fruit at the farmers' market in L.A., was always playing his old phonograph, and singing opera. He had a fair voice, not great but he put himself into it with passion. Luigi, his father's age, maybe older but full of music. Not deaf like his Dad, old Frank Nixon.

Now, as Dick dressed, he fumbled with buttons and cursed under his breath. Dick had no objection to hand-me-downs but he required a clean, starched white shirt every day. Dressing in the dark was possible. Keeping the lights off was the Eleventh Commandment around this house. "Electricity costs money," Dad would snap at any offender and turn off any light switch that Dick or his brother had reached up and clicked on, beginning when they first stood tall enough, years ago. Ma never turned on a light in her life. Wraith-like, quiet as a Quaker saint, Ma walked around the halls and rooms, even worked in the kitchen, curtains open for whatever moon or sun there was. Silently, she felt her way, with her gentle hands. It was spooky.

But Ma was not here. Dick's older brother, his hero, really, Harold, was dying in Arizona and Ma was with him. Dad remained at home with Dick, 17, and Donald, 15. Their accidental baby brother, Eddie, was with an aunt in Fullerton. Harold had TB. Harold, it seemed clear now to everybody, Harold was dying.

Dick brushed his teeth and washed carefully under his arm pits. Nothing disgusted him more than foul-smelling people or bad breath. Dick would smell garlic on Luigi's clothes and breath but it was not foul. Luigi and his son, Joey, were clean. The two men's long, black, curly hair was as clean as Dick's. The Italians were healthy, happy, lively. It showed in the way they moved, the way they talked.

Dick would eat an apple or a biscuit on the way, driving up on Route 101 to L.A., lights on, honking at any wobbling drunk drivers, watching to brake for dogs or cats or squirrels. The road sliced through the ugliest oil fields in California. He parked near Luigi's stand, and went there first.

"You look like the Devil," Luigi said, with an "a" at the end, as in "Devil-ah."

"No, you look like the Devil," Dick said.

Luigi did look like a stage devil, his eyebrows overgrown, and his hair wild and all over, he only needed horns. His smiling face and narrow chin with a goatee, he was strong-featured with big eyes and long eyelashes, all hands over everything, touch, touch, touch. Very Italian, Dick thought, never able to avoid a half-hug without seeming to be rude, enduring Luigi's touch.

Luigi's son, Joey, came in. A younger version of the old Devil.

"Late sleeper," Luigi said, pointing his thumb. "This gentleman," Luigi said, nodding, if not bowing, to Dick, "got up at four, and was on the truck before anybody, in here almost before the sun. And you?"

"And I got my rest, Pop," he said, breezily as could be.

Luigi hugged his boy and gave him a knuckle sandwich on his forehead.

"If I didn't love you," Luigi said. "Out on his date with Rosalina, this boy."

"I'm going to marry her, Pop," Joey said. "*Di noi arriva una coppia.*'"

Luigi laughed and explained to Dick yet one more time how his boy Joey, on his first date with Rosalina, had captured her attention – "and-a her heart-a" – by saying to her, in Italian, "we get to be a *coppia*, a couple someday."

Luigi was most interested that Dick played the piano.

"Music," Luigi said, both hands up like a conductor about to signal an orchestra, "is the salt of the world."

Dick laughed. Luigi meant "the salt of the earth," perhaps, but even that was not right. Luigi was no debater, nor was his son. Yet Dick never could get over their way of being a father and a son. Somehow, it seemed that Luigi could not be his father's age. Or that the son could not be his age. But they were.

Others did not try to do much conversing, let alone hugging, Dick. The Greek, the Armenian, one sly, the other sour, spared him very few words. Approaching truck farmers at the other stands, Dick would sample and bargain and pick until he had baskets of tomatoes, carrots, corn, cucumbers, lettuce, apples, sometimes walnuts and pistachios, sometimes grapes, and heft them up and pack them into the back of the truck, throw a tarp over everything and tie that down, then drive slowly back to Whittier.

Back at the store, curiously, Dad never offered or helped Dick unload the truck, placing fruits and vegetables in turn into a tub in back of the house, filling it with cold water and washing, then drying them with cloths. After he had stripped lettuce heads of any gritty outer leaves, and polished apples to shine, Dick took everything out front. Walking with heavy baskets in several trips, the fragile fruit and vegetables wavering and wiggling as he hauled them stiff-legged. Dick was on the football team but he was not strong and athletic. Once at the front of the store, rain or shine, under a green-and-white-striped awning that was getting a little faded with the sun and rain, stood home-made wooden boxes on legs for the vegetables and the fruits.

First, he had to reach in and get the soft, the broken, the rotten, and the maggoty and scoop these items up and chuck them.

Next, after going back and washing his hands, Dick brought long manila cards from off the shelf over the sink to write with a bold black marker the names of what he had and prices Dad had on his list. Leffingwell's lemon ranch was on one side of the store, the Murphy brothers' orange grove on the other, the smell of citrus hit him as he worked, more tart than sweet. He carried the unused cards and the oil-smelling marker back to the kitchen where late-sleeper Donald was now at the table at the chopping block with knives, trimming meats and putting them out on trays. They'd be off to school soon.

That night, after reading his schoolbooks until he was too tired and finding his way to bed, the sweetest music in the world to Dick was the wail of the train whistle as it went through Whittier at night and, when the wind came up from the south, the faint, rhythmic beats and creaks of the pumps of the oil patch on the road to Los Angeles. Since childhood, these sounds had evoked the outside world, places and people far away, connections. One exception was the Whittier Community Players, amateur theater in a town without live theater, a group that brought to life the scripts of playwrights of Broadway right here in Whittier. Dick, the former truck-driver to the farmers' market, now Mr. Nixon the attorney and counselor at law, wanted to be part of that now. And he wanted at last to be like Joey, telling a girl that someday they'd be a couple, someday he'd marry her. If Joey could win a girl's attention and her heart, Dick could, too. What worked for Joey could work for any young man with black hair.

CHAPTER TWENTY-SEVEN

Let's just suppose we juxtapose

"What about stream of consciousness?" Arlene asked me.

"Doing a James Joyce? With Dick Nixon and Pat? She wasn't Molly Bloom, yes, yes, oh, yes, and he wasn't Jewish. More of a Zippy the Clown as a sculpture by Alberto Giacometti," I said. "You know, external gloom over a naïve and here-now observer. These are not Joycean characters."

Arlene, bless her heart, argued with me. Her arms on each hip, standing enraged as an Irish washerwoman whose place I took in line, she faced me down.

"You can run with this ball, Gabe. By Saint Giacometti's Zippy, don't we all think in *non sequitars*, Gabe? And – Great Freud's Ghost, man -- about sex and improper thoughts, impolite stuff, swear-words and all, no matter who we are? So why would Dick and Pat be any different? In their mid-twenties, in Southern California, college grads, two professionals, a with-it, popular teacher and a lawyer carrying around self-pity, grievances and regret. What were their thoughts? Read their minds. Just do it."

"Well, Dick was an introvert. He'd be thinking about himself, his past, his present, his future, his alienation. Analyzing himself. Analyzing his analysis," I whined, begging off from trying.

"Deep."

"Deeper than Pat, and gloomier. Pat would be thinking: LaDonna is looking a little chubby, I wonder if John will try out, or Harry, and does this role require singing, I won't take it. But all the other teachers here are going to be in the play. I can't just walk out on them."

"I guess you can build on that instead," Arlene said, having shepherded me to the pasture she'd wanted to guide me to, I bet.

"If Dick worried that he'd fart, and eased his gas out without making a stink and was relieved by that, that's very human, very possible, and very credible but means nothing. Those thoughts are not going to be part of the story," I said, defining my bounds.

"They don't mean a fart," she said, agreeing.

"A fart would be all they mean," I said, insisting on the last word.

She obviously wanted to tease, if not torture, me.

"But didn't James Joyce have some character in *Ulysses* do voluntary penance and expiate his sins by breathing in the smell of stale urine? Isn't it possible that literature has only begun to exhaust the power of the human fart? Would you not be going where no artist fartist ever went before? The literary possibilities of the fart have not been nearly plumbed by fart jokes."

"Arlene! Give me something else."

"Pat never worried about her health."

Now, actually, that was something. *Yes*, as Molly Bloom said three times if she said it once. Health, Pat's health was remarkable: she denied the power of illness, a Christian Scientist without Margaret Baker Eddy.

"You're right, Arlene. Pat said that she did not get sick. Ever. And it was true. So, no, I don't think she thought that night: am I coming down with a cold? Or, maybe I'll get cancer. Those are thoughts that we all think, but no, not Pat."

"Isn't it amazing? That Pat was so healthy? And she never stressed about coming down with anything? She was like uncrowned royalty. Immune, exceptional, blessed. She believed in God, right? And that God divvied up the illnesses of the world?"

"She did believe in God. It was Dick who questioned the existence of a Deity."

"So, in your stream of consciousness, have Pat think happily about her special place among the few, maybe the only special one to whom God gave good health."

"No. You don't *dwell* on good health. If you have it, you don't think about health at all. It's a known fact."

"Then what *did* Pat think about?"

"Not herself. Others. The here-now, the church basement, LaDonna, the director, the play they'd be doing, a little bit. My earlier examples."

"Aha. Now you're cooking. They're in that basement for a play, a melodrama, an entertainment. Theater," Arlene said, smiling too smugly for me not to think: she wanted me to think this, she is manipulating me.

"No Nixon biographer or memoirist has yet elevated *The Dark Tower* to the height it actually enjoyed that night. They reduce it, anachronistically. But the play was the thing. I mean, that's why they were all together, technically. Didn't they read the script, evaluate its predicted reception, and think: how will this line be delivered? How will this scene go over in Whittier?"

"The play's the thing," Arlene said.

"The play's the thing. Barry Jones, the role Dick played, was a playwright who talked about other playwrights. What were they then? Playwrights within a playwright within a play. And a play had triggered an earthquake in Dick's life, a crisis of his life before and his life after the play," I said.

"What?" Arlene asked, although surely she knew at least the vague outlines of what I was about to say. She could hardly read anything about Dick's young manhood without reading and remembering Ola Welch. But I reviewed the story, the Story of Before That Night.

"Dick turned a Latin play of Aeneas and Dido back in high school into a six-year engagement off-stage with his co-star, Whittier girl Ola Welch. Ola expressly traced her affection for Dick back to that play. She did not like him before that. Afterwards, they were a couple. A platonic Hollywood marriage. This night in this church, beginning of the knitting together of an ensemble, a transient group, a gypsy tribe. Dick called Pat his Irish Gypsy. That is multi-layered, this getting a show together – Dick at his most spontaneous, without a thought about cares, health or tomorrow. That might reflect Dick's mood, a giddiness, gaiety, a touch of Ola, lost Ola, at least before the night ended, as the magical night of a second chance was ending."

"You could trace his thoughts from gloom to glad," Arlene said, nudging me to focus. I had a job to do: to write something. Thoughts?

"Dip into his thoughts, yes. A thought here and a contrasting thought there until you get a generally accurate impression of the flow of his thoughts that night. Nothing linear but Dick still would be more logical and coherent than most minds. He was always Mr. Rational. Pat was more of a puppy dog, thoughts all over the place."

"Okay, then. Not stream of consciousness for pages but dipping into their thought-stream and pulling out a trout now and then through the evening."

"Against a scripted background, literally, the relentless encouragement that everybody pay attention to this written text by two sophisticated New Yorkers, George S. Kaufman (who always wrote with somebody else, he never wrote alone) and Alexander Woollcott. Members of the Algonquin Round Table. The Algonquin Round Table began after the world war as a surprise roast of Woollcott, at which he had such fun that he suggested the same gang meet every week, which they did for years, adding wits as they went. Kaufman was one of the wits added later. There is no small irony in the association between California provincials Dick and Pat and the Algonquin Round Table of Manhattan."

"Which one was the most interesting, Kaufman or Woollcott?" Arlene asked.

"Definitely Woollcott," Gabe said, "The week before the audition, in January, 1938, Woollcott was just wrapping up his radio career. He had been the bell-ringing 'Town Crier.' He was a bachelor, people think it was because the mumps left him impotent. Lots of people thought his drama stank when he first tried writing plays. His nickname was 'Putrid.' Woollcott had to persevere against the odds, very Nixonian. Do you remember the movie 'The Man Who Came to Dinner?'"

"Yes, a classic. I've seen it on TV."

"Woollcott was the original for that character. He was 'The Man Who Came to Dinner.' He finally became a gloomy recluse, living alone on an island in a lake in Vermont. He died with six words on his lips, 'I never had anything to say.' I think somebody asked him if he had anything to say. Probably, he was just being witty. I hope to God he didn't die saying that *apropos* of nothing, and that depressed, dying like Chaucer, feeling useless and repenting of all of his works, especially *Canterbury Tales*. Woollcott's body was cremated and, as had been his wish, Woollcott's ashes were sent to his old college but they sent it to the wrong college and when the right college got them, they had to pay sixty-seven cents postage due."

"Definitely the most interesting one, but you can't use the story of Woollcott's ashes and postage due."

"No, I'm left with saying that the great Woollcott had just left the air and was no longer heard in Whittier homes or in any others as the town crier. I'll want to say it in a sad way, with gloomy words, so that it evokes an ominous note."

"I've got it already. 'Woollcott had no more to say on the air, Woollcott, who would say with his last breath that he never had anything to say, Woollcott the wit, Woollcott the critic, Woollcott the playwright, had fallen silent,' something like that," she suggested. "Then, 'If Woollcott's words were to move an audience in Whittier now, it was up to Dick and Pat.'"

"I don't know. But I know what you mean."

"What about Kaufman?"

"He was the only one who would live long enough to hear of Nixon. And to see Nixon defeated in 1960. He died in 1961. Woollcott died in 1943."

"When Nixon was playing poker and running 'Nick's Snack Shack' with the coldest pineapple juice in the Pacific for the Navy."

"Woollcott had a heart attack while he was on a panel discussion of the war. 'Germany is the cause of Hitler' were his last words on air. He was taken then to Roosevelt Hospital, where he died."

"1943."

"1943."

"Back to Kaufman."

"Back to Kaufman. Kaufman loved New York, hated sentimentality, was Jewish and said on live television, 'Let this be one Christmas show on which nobody sings 'Silent Night.' He had a wife and more women than you could shake a stick at. In 1938 he was awarded the Pulitzer Prize for drama, *You Can't*

Take It With You. Kaufman was the real brains behind *The Dark Tower*, he was the Broadway powerhouse. Cranky, sarcastic, bitter sometimes, you could say he had bad moods."

"A little Nixon there, too."

"A melodrama from the dark side, Arlene, I mean, what could be more appealing? For Pat, a change in emotional weather. For Dick, a moment to try on someone else's darkness."

"Did the play depict humanity as inherently evil? As in *film noir*?"

"Made into a movie starring Edward G. Robinson, somewhat cynical. If Dick trusted anybody, it was his mother. Maybe. Even then, we don't know, we can't be sure. But any play that showed people not trusting anybody and not being trustworthy would be meat and potatoes for Dick, who saw the world that way. Trust nobody. They will always bite your ass. Everybody betrays everybody. There are traitors in the State Department. And so forth. Dick made a career out of distrust. This play made money entertaining people with distrust."

CHAPTER TWENTY-EIGHT

Another country heard from

"Where did Dick's distrust of everybody come from?"

"The Holy Grail of Nixon studies," I told Arlene. "You know that, right?"

"I do now, if you say so."

"I do. Tom Wicker thinks somebody is out there or was out there who betrayed young Dick. Somebody he had so deeply trusted and been so deeply hurt by that he never trusted anybody else again."

"You don't think so."

"No. Not a person, not a chance. Dick would have talked. He would have taken revenge, even after he or she died, if he had no way in life."

"So what's your take?"

"His father," I said. "His father's fantasy, one that he swallowed whole and never forgot. When Frank Nixon married saintly Hannah Milhous, that family made him turn Quaker and stop swearing and get uncomfortably quiet. Of course, Frank never did get very quiet and he swore, as Dick would, when he was outside of hearing of any of the non-swearers."

"What's the fantasy?" Arlene said. I was glad to think that she was genuinely curious and that she viewed me as the font of knowledge. The Source of Nixon's Distrust. As if I actually held the keys.

"Frank was the one betrayed, in fantasy, Frank's own twist on history. How Frank Nixon was brought low. Frank imagined the lemon grove was a great deal, but he pinned that idea on old Milhous, thinking Milhous told him to buy it, take this money and buy that shithole. Nobody could make a living off that place. The old man made a fool out of Frank, with interest. Frank tried, getting angrier every year until he sold the damn place in 1922 at a loss and the best job he could find was in the oil fields outside Whittier, as a roustabout, bull labor. Oh, yeah, Dick heard a lot of times how Grandpa screwed Daddy, never trust anybody."

"And Dick had loved that town, Yorba Linda."

"In his memory, sure. In fantasy, it's Tom Sawyer's idyllic playground. Here, I have a note. This is how Dick described Yorba Linda, the town he was cheated out of at age seven because of his Grandpa's trick on his Daddy – 'In the spring the air was heavy with the rich scent of orange blossoms. And there was much to excite a child's imagination: glimpses of the Pacific Ocean to the west, the San Bernadino Mountains to the north, a 'haunted house' in the nearby foothills to be viewed with awe and approached with caution – and a railroad line that ran about a mile from our house.' Paradise or what? With a railroad line, though."

"Paradise. And then the Nixons fell into Whittier."

"And earned their bread by the sweat of their brow. Dick's Daddy was always quoting that bit of Scripture. Did you know? The Fall."

"Well," Arlene said. "Whittier seems to me not very different from Yorba Linda. Wasn't the store between a lemon grove and an orange grove?

"Oh, yes. Teasing, wasn't it? If you thought you should be in the citrus-growing farm area, to be stuck as a storekeeper between two groves, how would you feel?"

"So near and yet so far."

"Exactly. And it was not only that, Nixon's mother, the saint, took it hard. She never looked at Frank the same way again. Yorba Linda broke her down, she had to find a job at the Sunkist fruit factory, packing, bringing the boys with her."

"Really?"

"Sure, Dick helping out, sweeping floors for a few pennies."

"Like something out of Dickens."

"Worse, Dickens wrote about it, Dick kept it in. And his mother resented it all, never told any of them 'I love you.' Not once. Dick wove a verbal web around that sore point, I've read it, and how her eyes 'expressed love and warmth that no words could ever convey.' Ha. Ha and a half. Hah. The Fall devastated Hannah emotionally. She felt it as the Nixon Family Fall from independent yeomanry in Eden down into sweat labor, first in Yorba Linda, then in Whittier."

"Because of her father?"

"In fantasy, Arlene."

"But perception is everything, as Nietzsche said."

"Yeah. In fantasy, as Dick perceived it, mean old Milhous set a trap for poor, innocent Frank to fall into. Again, note the railroad. The funny thing is that in this Paradise the little boy was always listening to train-whistles at night and thinking of going other places – like anyplace – and, hey, I forgot the best part. Dick got a legend to grow in his head, totally bogus, it took over, like this was real, that the Nixons would have been millionaires if they'd only held onto that lemon grove a little bit longer, as oil was discovered on it."

"No oil?"

"Not a drop. Totally made-up fictional story to compound what Daddy lost, Paradise and a million dollars. Verbal revenge. Dick made it up – unconscious revenge – to stab old, dead Milhous so he indirectly lost a million bucks from the trick he played on Dick's father. Turning the trap story into the biter bit."

"Wow. Busy unconscious. Busy revenge-seeking unconscious."

"You know Dick's father, as he knew him, was a terrible bully, a loud, barking dog of a man, quick-tempered. Dick kept on his good side and tried to get his brothers to cater. Big Oedipal thing that Dad might kill him. Threw the boys into a drainage ditch when they sailed boats or went too close, a relative yelled for him to stop, afraid they'd drown. 'You'll kill them, Frank.' Imagine hearing that as you're struggling, dog-paddling. A woman in real fear. Might screw you up for life."

"But he didn't blame his father."

"No, he spun. It all went back to the myth of the Milhous betrayal. He probably thought about it every day, getting up at four."

"Four?" Arlene said. "You're kidding, right?"

"No, really. He got up at four in the morning for years -- and you know how teen-agers crave sleep -- to get into a truck and hit the road for the Seventh Street farmers' market in L.A., to beat the farmers and wholesalers down on prices and to grab the freshest fruit and vegetables to resell at a mark-up in the family store in Whittier. It took him a half-hour there, a half-hour back, an hour to pick and bargain, another hour at home to wash, to sort, and to arrange the produce on the stands in front of the store. Then it was eight o'clock and off to school."

"Heavy labor, sweat of his brow labor he had to do because of his father marrying Hannah."

"Now you're cooking, Arlene. Wouldn't that give you a dark side? Distrust? Especially distrust of your father-in-law. The moral of this fantasy story was a strong, clear message to Dick to be real careful about who he marries."

"How's that?"

"Watch out for her *father*. Make sure he's a solid, reliable man of his word and that he likes you."

"Ola. The police chief's daughter. Dick got along famously with the father."

"And nobody else. Ola's mother couldn't stand him, but Dick could care. Ola's *mother* was not the danger."

"But, Gabe, Pat was an orphan. When they met in 1938."

"No fath-er, no dan-ger," I said, making two syllables carry the water of my meaning. "Arlene, the coast was clear."

"Wow."

"Her old man was not going to screw him, the father angle was secure. Pat was a prize, a rose without thorns in having no living father. And then there was the link to theater."

"Tell me."

"I quote Adlai Stevenson, 1956, 'This is a man of many masks; who can say they have seen his real face?' John Kennedy during the 1960 campaign, 'I feel sorry for Nixon because he doesn't know who he is, and at each stop he has to decide which Nixon he is at the moment, which has to be exhausting.' And, when Herb Butterfield told the Ervin Committee about the Watergate tapes, he explained, 'The President is very history-oriented and history-conscious about the role he is going to play.' It was all-the-world-a-stage mentality, with self-consciousness about playing roles. The best bluffer at the poker-table in the Navy. Street theater for profit. Before the second debate with Kennedy, he admitted in his book, *Six Crises*, that he decided sincerity would work. He said that he decided, quote, what was most important was that I be myself, unquote. Putting on a new act as oneself. Whew. Arlene,

Nixon was an actor's actor. He took to theater like a fish to water or a cat to cream."

"Or me to you."

"Or me to you, baby. Forget taping for history, Oedipus in his old age remembered in his memoirs the parts that he'd played in college productions. He lingered lovingly over having been successful as 'the dithering Mr. Ingoldsby in Booth Tarkington's *The Trysting Place*, the Innkeeper in John Drinkwater's *Bird in Hand*, an old Scottish miner in a grim one-act play, *The Price of Coal*, and a rather flaky comic character in George M. Cohan's *The Tavern*.' Notice anything?"

"He's got a good memory almost fifty years later for shows he was in."

"He recalls the roles, the playwrights and the plays."

"He liked acting."

"He *really* liked acting. And theater. When he was in New York looking for a job after law school, in the renewed Depression of 1937, with almost no money, he went to see *Tobacco Road*. And more --."

"A theater buff."

"A fan, as in fanatic."

"People in Whittier must have noticed."

"At least one did. When she found a play including a prosecutor, Ayn Rand's *The Night of January 16th* – curious title, isn't it?"

"What?"

"It's the real title, why?"

"The books are all so specific that Dick met Pat on January 18, 1938. January 16 was a Sunday that year, not a good day for a church basement audition in a Sabbath-respecting Quaker town. Authors may have felt January 16 should be January 18, and silently corrected it."

"Wait, here's RN, Nixon's memoirs," Gabe said. "Oh, my. You're right. He does not have a date, he has them meeting later in 1938. In early 1938 he says that he got a call from LaDonna Baldwin to play the prosecutor in Ayn Rand's play, *The Night of January 16th*."

"Yeah. It wasn't January, let alone January 18, 1938."

"Couldn't be January 18, that's the month that the director of the Whittier Community Players, LaDonna Baldwin, called Dick, the new lawyer, who only started up with Tingle and Mewley in mid-November, six or eight weeks earlier, and asked him if he'd be interested in the role. He did it, well, of course."

"It was in character for him."

"Was it ever? So the next audition, when it came – Julie Nixon says February, based on Pat, Dick in RN says months after January but he gave no month anyway – it was not a distinct anniversary to Dick and Pat -- not invited this time, Dick dropped by."

"And met Pat."

"So he says, here, from his memoirs: 'I thought I knew everyone in Whittier, but that night a beautiful and vivacious young woman with titian hair appeared whom I had never seen before. I found I could not take my eyes away from her. This new girl in town was Pat Ryan, and she had just begun teaching at Whittier High School. For me it was a case of love at first sight."

"Ewcc, that phrase 'for me.' As in, for me but *not* for her, as in Pat did not fall in love with poor me then, it took me a long time to make her love poor me, her lover at first sight."

"There is also this about Pat: 'She decided to adopt the name her Irish father' – remember, Dick's father was an 'Irish father,' – 'liked to call her, and became known to everyone as Pat. It is deeply irritating to be burdened with a name you dislike…'"

"He kind of thought that his daughters would not like any name the parents gave them."

"Pat suggested giving the girls only one name, no middle name, to make it easy, 'so they could change them or add to them when they were old enough to decide.'"

"She'd gone to a tech school of Columbia in New York, and night school at University of Southern California, working 40 hours a week as a research assistant for a professor. She did other jobs, including two stints on screen in Hollywood films. She was not educated in law, but she was very well educated and experienced, all on a shoestring, making the most of every opportunity and making opportunities where there were none, none at all."

CHAPTER TWENTY-NINE

The long arm of the law

"What about his last client?" Arlene said after we had refreshed our acquaintance over all obstacles.

"His last client?" I asked.

Arlene said, "Someone had to be the last client Dick talk to before he went to the audition, the one whose case he would be thinking about, as he had a perfect memory for facts, mulled them over and constantly thought about business. That case, that client would have been big in his mind that night."

"Hmm. But what would be the point?"

"A divorce case. A woman seeking to divorce her husband."

"Oh," I said. "I think I know now where this is headed."

"You do," Arlene said, closing her eyes and shaping a grotesque, exaggerated smile on her lips as she responded, saying, "Sexual secrets. Intimacies of the boudoir. Frank talk. In coarse words. The woman who told her sexual secrets as Dick turned a trillion shades of purple or something. He wrote about it in his memoirs and he told someone in an interview. It's famous, how he asked Mewley not to do any more divorce cases."

"What amazed him was that they weren't embarrassed and they never ceased to make their complaints about their men in that department," I said.

"And he hated that, as he is writing down euphemisms for the vernacular words, Latin, and he is blushing and resenting. But he had to listen."

"So," I said. "He'd be stewing over, twitching, kicking and fidgeting with frustration over an impossible situation not only of being some slut's lawyer but having to look up whether it is cruel and abusive treatment, grounds for divorce, if a man did this or that in the bedroom."

"Yes. Call Josh."

"Why?"

"He's a lawyer, isn't he? He can tell us what they hear or deal with."

"Massachusetts is a no-fault state, irreconcilable differences is enough. You don't have to get into the sex stuff anymore, or prove adultery like you used to, with detectives and photographs."

"Call him anyway. Maybe he has some historical cases he can talk about."

I did, and got to the meat of the matter quickly.

"I'm looking for a plausible case that really could have happened that would have tormented a prudish, inhibited, private gentlemanly lawyer," I told Josh.

"I suppose adultery."

"Of course, but how would it be a torture?"

"Well, you made me think of the definition and proof in court. For adultery, you had to have sexual intercourse. The male member, call him Willy, had to penetrate the female pudenda, call her Ethel. If you had sex without that, if Willy did not enter Ethel, it was not adultery. It was sex, sure – but not adultery."

"Why was that?" I said. "A blow job is not adultery?"

Josh explained, "Adultery was considered a sin against the reproductive capacity, the exclusive rights to make a child with the woman. It was assumed, it was known, by the practical judges who decide cases that the cats would play, male and female, and get off on all sorts of things, but the one thing was they did not want any poor bugger to have to support some other man's child. That was the no-no."

"And so no intercourse, no child."

"That's right, professor. You could come up to the gates but no farther. Or is it further?"

"No father, I think."

"That would be important, for the woman to say that she knew her husband got a blow job or a hand job or anything but the real deal, Willy meets Ethel, it would not hold up in court. So to speak."

I thanked Josh and fleshed out the call, so to speak, in detail to Arlene.

"You have your ideal client interview now," Arlene said. "All sorts of sex thoughts and scenarios running through Dick's head when he sees this fantasy woman walk in that night. With whom he might be on stage. Oooh."

"I can't get over it," I said.

"What?"

"Clinton was right. A blow job doesn't count. He did not have sex with that woman. In a legal sense."

"Your view of history just changed?"

"History is the story of how the past keeps changing."

"What is fiction?"

"Anything short of intercourse that brings pleasure, my love."

I began to write, starting with big capital letters underlined, knowing that whatever followed would only be a first draft:

REWRITE

Dick remembered the scare, the spot over his right lung, thinking TUBERCULOSIS and I'M GOING TO

DIE for three months, until another x-ray finally showed it was nothing, "*just an old scar from pneumonia years ago*" – Dick had almost died from pneumonia when he'd been four -- no concern or care in the doctor's voice, *just, just, just, just an old scar from pneumonia just an old scar from pneumonia just an old scar from pneumonia.*

I'm not going to die. Arthur died but I'm going to live. In their silent house where everybody was so private and didn't even pray out loud, except that his father yelled and argued, yelled and argued all the time, half-deaf Dad, Dick went to his mother. Dad had been yelling, as usual about politics but the past few weeks it was always condemning "crooked lawyers." The Attorney General and his staff had been identified as fraudsters and con men on a large scale, selling oil leases to private companies, sacrificing Navy reserves to line their own pockets. Dick was shaken by the idea that the sort of lawyers Dad appreciated were getting scarce, that the world had changed dark and evil. He came to his saintly mother to make his vow: "*I'm going to be an old-fashioned kind of lawyer, a lawyer who can't be bought.*" He, Dick, if he had a whole life ahead of him after all, he better make plans, he better get himself ready to do great things and great things, big problems to solve were in all the newspapers, a White House scandal, crooked deals in oil leases, that only came out after President Harding died.

"You'll be like Attorney Mewley then," Ma told Dick. Ma thought it was wishful fancy and vain hope. Seeing his expression, Ma said with earnestness, "I'll pray for it, Dick."

Now, Ma's prayers had been answered. Dick *was* an attorney, working in Attorney Mewley's office, with a secretary and everything. He was meeting with a client in the "consultation room" that was the little library of Tingle & Mewley.

He was nervous and skittish in front of strangers, nothing had thawed out his generally stiff comportment. Mewley joked that Dick should relax. "You're not in the Army," he'd say. "At ease. I've never seen anybody so stiff."

"You look awfully uncomfortable in that chair," his client said. She was Charlotte -- "my legal name is Charlotte but call me Carlotta, honey."

Dick, in his straight-backed wooden chair of unforgivingly straight lines, told her, "I find that one does one's best work uncomfortable, ma'am."

She nodded.

"One does? This one doesn't. I do my best work lying down," she said, laughing as Dick blushed. "I'm a dish, aren't I, Dick?"

"We have to name grounds for divorce. Was he cruel and abusive to you?"

"Well, he left me high and dry many a time, if you call that cruelty," she said, laughing open-mouthed. "You know what I mean? You wouldn't do that to a girl, would you? One that did her best to please you?"

"I'm sorry not to understand you."

"You understand my words but not my meaning, pretty boy?"

He blushed again.

"Don't you blush," she said. "You are just the sweetest. I never met a man like you. And smart, too, I bet."

Dick sometimes slept the night on the couch in this room, a couch this woman seemed to be eyeing every few minutes herself. Here he sat, back in Whittier, after having graduated third in his class at Duke, traveled to Manhattan, applied at two firms, both of which interviewed him before sending regretful information of their lack of a position to offer him. He had dropped into an office in LA and left his application to become an FBI Agent. Only when nothing came of that, too, did he return Attorney Mewley's call.

"My husband used to run the café on the corner of East Street and Perkins."

"Oh," Dick said, knowing exactly where she meant.

She said, "You closed it down."

"Not exactly."

"Yes, you did. You ran the place out of business very cleverly."

"They had no license to sell liquor."

"True," she said. "But you knew that they could apply unless there was a history. And you made a history."

Dick blushed.

"You had a cop stationed across the street to arrest all the customers coming out drunk, which was all of them. You put them in jail and not one of them would ever go back to that café. Which now had a history of trouble and closed down."

She stubbed out her cigarette, applied lipstick in an interesting languid way, and then said, "As soon as this divorce is done, I'm going to Miami. You like to come, Dick?"

She laughed salaciously.

"I don't see the point of beach days," Dick said, his anger spilling over now. "I've seen people who laze their lives away, just lying around, you know, in the sun or under an umbrella. Usually drinking. I cannot think of a sight more pitiful."

"Well, then I'll send you a post card, dearie, and you can pity *me*."

He inhaled noisily through his nose and then sighed with an equal rudeness before completing the interview. Once she left, he was ready to audition. Back in the world of civilized. He'd ask Mewley: no more divorces. Life was a battle.

CHAPTER THIRTY

Nailing it

Three shrinks walk into a scriptorium. Why do I find this book last? The shrinks have analyzed Nixon including childhood, rejections and chasing Pat around. They nailed him.

"I can't write another word," I told Arlene.

"Why now?"

"They beat me to it. They got him down on paper, published years ago. Twentieth century."

I showed her their book and she flipped through it but she didn't flip. She gave the book back to me, caressed my wrist and said, "Your book is different."

"Different title, sure."

"No. They're psychiatrists, they're scientists. You come with language to expose Parolles. A creature of words."

"They *know* he was a word man," I said. "Look, they cracked the eternal mystery of why Dick didn't destroy the tapes, the Watergate tapes. They were his words. He valued his words, they were him. For him to burn his tapes would have been to erase himself, a sort of verbal suicide. No way, he wanted them. They were going to be speaking for him long after he was dead. And they are."

"You are the only word man I'd ever want to keep."

"You going to keep me?"

"Stay, o moment so fair."

"Faust."

"After speaking about the glory of work."

"Draining the salt marshes of the North Sea."

"Making fertile and fruitful what had been a barren waste."

"Fertile and fruitful? My book?"

"Your novel. From blank, barren sheets of paper. Hey, the shrinks just wrote a book. You, my friend, are writing a novel."

"All by myself, yeah."

"You will crack this nut with just your imagination, your powerful questions and your flood of freshwater, cleansing words. You will flush him out. Dick will be caught on the wing, in motion, on stage, in that car, a fluid and live picture of the guy at that time, with that girl, Pat, as she was."

"You think so?"

"No, I think you should just quit and not do this project, it's beyond you, total waste of time. You're right."

"I'm not right. You're right."

"No, you're right."

"I'm not right, you're right."

We kept that up until we were both laughing too hard to keep it going. Probably nobody ever laughed harder or longer at the idea that writing up Dick meeting Pat was a hoot and a half, which it surely was. And, through Arlene, I saw: it was not beyond me to do this.

Gabe read the shrinks' description, with eyewitness quotes that, while dating Ola, Dick had been combative rather than conciliatory, exhibiting the same nasty temper that his father showed at home. He used to storm out in a huff, then return the next day as if nothing had happened. Weirdly, although he wrote Ola from Duke for more than a year, nobody at Duke knew that he had a girl back home. Mum was the word. Dick knew all about close-mouthed omission to disclose, and distraction from anything he chose to conceal. It was Quaker privacy metastasized.

Best of all, they had a blockbuster suggestion about Dick's telling Pat, "Don't laugh! Someday I'm going to marry you!" They said, with equal exclamation: ""The outburst was so unlike Nixon's usual calculating decision-making that, in light of his prior experience with Ola Welch, one might wonder whether he had planned even before meeting Pat how he would propose to any girl!"

These experienced, prolific and scholarly psychs, standing on their clinical experiences, offered a window to look at Dick as a walking, talking, and prepared proposer. "It is possible that at this time in his life," they said, "Nixon experienced an internal urgency to find a mate..."

Pat, they said, struck him as himself in female form: a self-reliant, determined, bit aloof free spirit. Thus, the onset of a long and largely unrequited chase after her. Where he had done the daily rejecting and keep-away moves with Ola, he played the role of the one rejected or kept away as Pat did the rejecting and pushing in the relationship he imposed upon them both.

At a speech to the National Football Foundation in 1969, Dick wanted a good story or, more aptly, a reason – even a bogus one -- to recite his recollection of a game between Duke and USC. He brought in Pat. Duke had lost that game, Dick said her was terribly disappointed "but the woman who was to be my future wife went to Southern Cal and that is how it all worked out. We met at that game."

Thus toppling *The Dark Tower.*

CHAPTER THIRTY-ONE

I scream, you scream

Arlene without an appetite was not the Arlene I knew but here we sat together at our ice-cream parlor. We did not have an "our song," or "our poem," or "our anything" but we did have our ice-cream parlor in Harvard Square. Here we could, each of us, think back with vivid nostalgia of ice-cream sundaes with hot fudge or caramel sauce, cherries or not, jimmies, mix-ins like oreos and (though I hated them, she loved them on sweet cream) little jelly bears. Or double-scoop frappes, malted. Oh, heaven. Cinnamon spice ice-cream in a dish all by itself.

Today was different.

Today Arlene looked down at her ice-cream, a masterpiece of M & M's over hot fudge over totally-flooded-and-no-doubt-half-melted vanilla bean, on top of a warm brownie with walnuts.

"Are you ill?" I asked.

"I think so."

Whoa. Arlene was never, ever ill.

"Have you seen a doctor?"

"Yes," she said, now looking me in the eyes.

"You have?" I said, less assured than accusingly. She had not told me.

"I didn't want you to worry," she said. "Not until you were out of the hospital."

What?

"How long ago was it that you saw a doctor?"

"Look, Gabe," she said, reaching out to touch my hand, the foolish hand holding a foolish white plastic spoon. Thank God, I did not pull my hand away. I feel that's important to say. No matter how upset I was, I did not pull my hand back. She touched me, and pressed her cool hand onto mine, then grasped my hand and squeezed as if to infuse understanding into me. "I have leukemia. I've had it for about six months, the doctor thinks. But I've been too busy to think."

"Or do anything about it. What do they recommend? Have you had tests? Is this confirmed or are they still guessing? Doctors can be wrong, you know."

"I did a confirming test and got a second opinion. And I have my own opinion, that I am pretty sick. I could eat until yesterday but now that's gone. I can hardly look at food."

"Let's get out of here," I said.

She didn't oppose the idea and we walked out of the placer, our place. I glanced back at the table of two dishes of ice-cream and spoons and napkins. That sight remains, for me, the illustration of The Story of When Arlene Said She Was Sick.

Outside, in the fresh air and busy bodies of bopping, hopping Harvard Square, we found a bench. Nobody seemed sick at that moment, not even Arlene. I don't know which of us spoke, or what we said, or if we said anything, sitting there in the sun. I remember holding her, worrying I was crushing her, thinking she might be frail if she was sick. And thinking: I can't lose this woman, who is my life. Besides the ice-cream parlor, I realized that there was one other "our" and that was "our future." We had spent a lot of time talking about it, constructing it, dreaming it vaguely and specifically, continually inserting new pipes and sections to this great machine that would take us both From Now On. I'm sure we did not talk about the future, I can't imagine that we talked about anything of the past and, of the present, she had already said everything that needed to be said. I think we put off thinking altogether, and talking, and only felt one another, embracing and kissing. Some passersby might have been amused by the couple making out so publicly on a bench in Harvard Square. Be our guests, be amused. If love amuses you, so be it. Love is the most important thing that happens to us human beings. We, creatures of animated stardust who eventually get sick and die, have our course and only rarely two of us collide into a course together. The only question then is: how long, o Lord, how long?

CHAPTER THIRTY-TWO

If You Wanna Be Happy

The first thing I tried one morning was imagining a speech Dick may have written and delivered, had he returned to Whittier to commemorate the fiftieth anniversary of *The Dark Tower* in 1988:

Fellow enthusiasts of amateur theater,

I once had a role in a play. You know, my family life had diminished as I moved across the road to live alone in a room I rented over my father's garage. Each two weeks, after Mr. Mewley gave me my money (my share as the associate at Tingle and Mewley), I gave my father five dollars for rent and five dollars to repay him for small sums he had sent me when I had been a student at Duke Law School. On those occasions, of course, my mother would insist that I sit with them and my two brothers, Don and Ed, for some of her stew and pie, usually apple. She always gave me some to take home, too.

Now, my brother, being as unmarried as I was and having some money set aside, joined with me to purchase an automobile, a used car, a 1935 Chevrolet. There was nothing wrong with it, by the way, which was good because I was never handy. What I was good at besides debating was reading and memorizing, two skills vital to actors. On that basis LaDonna Baldwin, the director of the Whittier Community Players, selected me for the role of Barry Jones in The Dark Tower.

Now, as I recall, three or four Whittier High School teachers were also selected that night by Mrs. Baldwin, one of them being Pat Ryan. Pat's stature among us amateurs was high. Pat had had success in Hollywood. Besides experience as an extra in two films, she was the most beautiful woman that I had ever seen off-screen.

I want to make it clear that I had not seen Pat before, although I knew everybody in Whittier. At the evening's end, I offered Elizabeth Cluett a ride home. She and I had dated a couple of times. Liz asked if I would mind also driving Pat home, it being on the way. They both won a ride home, an uneventful ride as rides go, no traffic, no sudden swerves, and no close calls. I drove that night as I always drove, safely and, if anything, slowly. I obeyed the laws.

Pat's home came along first, a bungalow she rented with another woman. As I dropped her off, I asked when she would give me "a real date."

Pat answered that she was very busy, which I took as a challenge. I was not prepared to give up, you see. I understood instantly that this was a moment of failure that I could salvage. What I said then, however, still surprises me all of these years later. I said, "You've got to give me a date because I'm going to marry you."

Now, why I said that, mentioning marriage on the first occasion of our meeting, has been a source of speculation ever since, including, I must say, my own. There are three reasons:

First, it was unlike me to telegraph any sort of emotion or romantic interest. Moreover, in this case Elizabeth Cluett was present and she heard everything.

Second, I knew – and Pat confirmed this to me later – that, for Pat, one simply did not joke when it came to marriage. She looked at me very sharply when I brought it up.

Third, and the most contrast of all, I was a rational planner and never an impulsive or spontaneous speaker.

All of these factors considered, I can only suggest that a sixth sense was operating.

In summary, there is no doubt that this audition changed my own life and the lives of several others.

Dissatisfied, I crumpled these pages up and threw them away and I tried again:

Dick lacked a wife.

"You need a wife, Dick," his father said to him as they stood together in the store, Dad treating him to a Coca-Cola. Had he been another sort of man or a different father, he might have said something about speaking from experience or meaning no criticism. But Frank Nixon being Frank Nixon, he said it loud, as deaf people sometimes do, and expected no disagreement from Dick.

Dick, turning the last of his drink bottoms up preparatory to going across the street and upstairs to his room over the garage, where he would shower, change clothes and maybe go out or maybe just read, never argued with Dad. They were both great arguers. Dick made a name as a debater in every school he ever attended -- but not by arguing with his father, whom he urged his brothers to leave to his own opinions. Don and Edward did not argue with Dick but neither did they take his advice. Dick could sometimes hear them arguing from across the street.

As to a wife, Dick had tried and failed to lure Ola Florence without success. Dick had her old man's vote, the police chief, but her mother would never come around, never said much and Ola told him that her mother was always nitpicking what he wore and the way he talked, how no Nixon would ever make a good husband. Apparently, although Ola was too polite to say it, Dick's father was the example of a bad husband, one who was grouchy, stingy, narrow-minded and just not husband material. Perhaps, had Ola's sister, Dorothy, liked him, he'd have carried the day but even Dorothy, well, followed her mother. Dick sent a silver candy dish to Ola as a wedding gift, and wished them all the best. Lately, to his friends, he'd send three wedding gifts thinking, each time, when would his time come to be on the receiving end. Not that Dick wanted silver candy dishes or any of the stupid things he was sending, he just thought fair was fair.

Everybody Dick worked with at the office was married, the secretary was married, old Mewley was married, and they were not unhappy, although they were not cooing about and tripping lightly like honeymooners. On the other hand, the married clients Dick talked with – and they spoke far too intimately, too casually about sex than Dick thought was right – were examples of marriages gone wrong, dead or dying partnerships regretted by both the man and the woman.

"Try and get back together, can't you?" Dick would ask. After all, although not all clients appreciated this, it was a lawyer's duty to encourage reconciliation. One woman laughed in his face and, having spent thirty minutes running down her husband, whom Dick perceived only as an inoffensive, well-intentioned man, actually shouted at him, "You understand English, right? What I told you? The man's a jerk to me and always has been." Rather than feeling the gravity of the legal step she was about to take, she seemed to want to get back on the hunt again for somebody better. In the pit of his stomach, Dick felt so nauseous so often in those conferences that he'd asked Mewley to assign him only oil leases, criminal cases and wills.

So he should marry?

"To the right woman," that was the key. Who would make him happy? What sort of woman would he, in turn, make happy? Well, she'd have to be serious about life and be willing to take risks, certainly, and be at home in public, up on a platform. Dick was going to be a politician, he had his eye on a seat in the Assembly and already neighbors approaching him to help. None of them said it but he knew that a wife helped on the campaign trail.

The right woman for him to please would be a good talker, an intelligent woman, certainly a college graduate. And she would not be unaware of his dark black hair and regular looks. Dick looked at himself in the mirror to straighten his tie before work, to make sure his hair was in place, he practiced expressions for debates and court and the imaginary campaign, and he thought generally he looked presentable. He would never be Tarzan, his build was on the slight side, but he was not unathletic. If she liked to ice skate, say, he could take that up. If she bowled, he knew how, not well, but he knew how to avoid the gutter.

What was he looking for? If she were to have golden-red hair and blue eyes and a slightly freckled, high-cheek-boned face with a broad smile, slim, even willowy, why, that'd be okay, too. She didn't have to be a cover girl or a screen star but she should not be a downcast Olive Oil in eyeglasses and a frown, either, no matter how serious, intelligent and comfortable on stage she might be.

Tonight he would not stay home. Although LaDonna had not called him specially this time to invite him to try out, Dick would go to the audition for the Whittier Community Players. Maybe Elizabeth Cluett would be there, she was sort of sparky, he could always invite her out. There were fish in the littler pond that formed sleepy Whittier, and the liveliest ones went to auditions. Maybe he would meet a nice girl in the auditions. He knew every girl in Whittier. But some co-ed from out of town might walk a block over from the college. Who knew?

Dick made it a point to analyze what went wrong. He decided that he was too self-conscious. Maybe he could not change that, he could never reduce his awareness and turn into a dullard. He was always going to be a perceptive person. But he could act, he could adopt a stage persona in debate and he would apply that in life. If he met a girl tonight, he would be a devil-may-care, he would ask her out on a date but not in his usual hyper-aware way, all eyes and nervous, too intense. No, he'd say, "How about it, kid?" and she'd ask how about what, and he'd say, "Can we go out this Saturday?" Or, why strong it out, "When are you going to give me a date?" Yes, sure. What did he have to lose anyway? When are you going to give me a date?

What then?

She might say no. So? So then, how about "How am I ever going to marry you if you don't give me a date?"

Totally great, a whole new vista. He did not have to talk with a girl as he did when addressing the court or in talking with a political group. Keep it light, funny, even wild and crazy. That's what girls like. Ola probably liked it but Dick only had his earlier limited awareness. He grew on self-consciousness, analyzing and re-analyzing until everything became clear. Then he changed, he improved and, little by little, he was a coveted date. Not yet, not even tonight, but he'd practice on some girl. Tonight. He had at least one thing that not every man had in 1938: a car, and not too old a car, either. Dick could offer a ride home in his shiny brown 1935 Chevy. And say at the ride's end, "When are you going to give me a date?"

When are you going to give me a date, he practiced, in a casual, off-hand, flippant way, with a smile, a really toothy grin.

Dick found his way to the Sunday school room, the walls of which were covered by children's artistic efforts to visualize God, angels, Christ on the cross, Noah's Ark and other Bible stories. It would not be confused with the Sistine Chapel, but its ever-new view of a world new to young eyes made script-reading seem a tedious exercise. Would it be worth it? He would see. Oh, yes, he would see. LaDonna thanked Dick for coming, said that she was so glad to see he'd come to try out and gave him a script to study, asking him to study "Barry's" lines.

"The Dark Tower" by George S. Kaufman and Alexander Woollcott. Dick flipped through pages to find "Barry," Barry Jones in the list of characters. Page after page, no Barry. Then a line:

"How does one curry favor with you, Miss Temple?"

Jesus. And it was a minor role. Barry Jones the supposed playwright – who changed his name to Barry from Horace for never-explained reasons – he should have changed Jones -- only appeared for a few lines late in Act 1, then totally vanished until another cameo in Act 3 with Daphne. Their return to the stage in Act 3 is, however, obviously intended to be stunning, a tableaux for a pair, a duo, a team, partners greeted with the immortal words, "Jones & Martin, card tricks and sex appeal."

One imagines the hoots, cheers and applause as Barry and Daphne stand side by side, if not arm in arm, the ideal couple on display. Barry stands mute as Daphne natters and banters away. This Daphne dame would be a good role for somebody, Daphne Martin, the hard-drinking, tough-talking star from her first line. In Act 1, she comes out with a shocker, the interrupted, "The son-of-a-" followed by, "I beg your pardon. I didn't catch the end of that." Daphne says, "I'll give you three guesses."

Daphne would also sing "Stormy Weather" as Barry played the piano, plus the World War One favorite "A Long, long Trail A-Winding."

He hoped Daphne would be The One. He would enjoy rehearsal time with Daphne. And Act 2 they would be backstage, waiting together for the cue to make their grand second entrance on stage. Backstage, behind the curtains, a couple in waiting.

He studied Barry further and found that the schmuck, in his longest series of lines, defended youthful achievers on stage. "Young? I'm twenty-four. Noel Coward was only twenty-three when he wrote 'The Vortex.'" Barry goes on, spouting that Sheldon wrote "Salvation Nell" when he was only twenty-two, topped by a character who stifles him by saying, "And Chatterton was only eighteen when he hanged himself."

Then Dick spotted a real tongue-twister, his only really long line, spoken to the star of the show: "I guess I did sound pretty complacent. I can't help being tickled about the business, but don't think I don't know it's all due to you. Why, I'd rather have you in my play and have it play to empty benches than have anybody else in it and have it a success."

Duck soup. Dick had a near-photographic memory, never forgot what he read, reciting minutes-long poems even in first-grade of a length that adults could not believe they would ever remember. Dick imagined the eternity that this line would live in his skull, ever ready to be recited, whether in 1938 or in 1968.

CHAPTER THIRTY-THREE

Fellow, Follow Bellow

"Saul Bellow."

"Yes."

"Walking to work in Paris, which he hated, but he'd won a Guggenheim and his wife loved Paris. Bellow sees the city cleaners flushing the streets, you know, gushing water, fluid. It looks better than anything in Paris to him. Running water. He thinks, 'I want the freedom of running water,' something like that. Immediately, shazam, the novel he is working on goes poof. Disappears. He knows it's poison. Pop, into his head pops his childhood friend, a boy named Charles August. He morphs quickly into Augie March."

"Bellow's breakthrough."

"His breakthrough novel. As Bellow told it, he only had 'to be there with buckets to catch it.' That running water, you see? It poured down onto him."

"What's Saul Bellow got to do with anything?"

"Nothing directly."

"Nothing. It has nothing to do with Nixon and what you're writing."

"I'd like a glass of water, please."

"Running water?"

"The runniest."

As she unscrewed the top of a small bottled water, and poured it into a styrofoam cup for him, she asked Gabe, "Are you thinking that you hate the Nixon contest? That it's poison?"

"I can't figure it out yet."

After a pause, and a sip, he said, "Maybe."

They said nothing more for a good five minutes.

"You know what's funny?" Gabe asked.

"Are you done with your water?" she asked.

He was and she took his cup and put it into the plastic-lined wastebasket, much smaller than any they had at home.

"They never talked about the past. I mean, we talk about the past, don't we? Our childhood, school, anecdotes, you know, old friends and things that hurt us or made us feel great."

"All the time."

"They didn't. Pat and Dick lived for the future and talked about it. Not just what they wanted but how they were going to get there. The past was only a fleeting part of the running account, bases they'd already touched on the way, punches on the ticket they didn't have to worry about again."

"Weren't their futures different? I mean, Pat was thinking of independence, being a successful woman, moving on up after teaching, probably. Not the movies but something solid. And she could do it."

"Yeah, futures in conflict. That was the trouble from the beginning. Dick's overall political dream was okay but he'd weave into it loving her and marrying her and she rebelled. She let him blahblahblah on about current events, issues, criticism of Democrats, muted praise of a few programs – Social Security they both approved of – and Republican remedies and cures for urgent problems. I mean, in 1938 there were plenty of problems to discuss solving."

"Hitler."

"To name only one. But Dick was dead in the present, caught up in the future. He was a spider spinning a web, networking an organization to come forward whenever he threw his hat into the ring to fight his way into the Assembly."

"He was never in the Assembly."

"It was the first office he expected, and was encouraged to aspire to by Herman Perry, a power broker in Whittier. Dick went to Washington and then into the Navy so his first office, skipping the Assembly to keep on schedule for the White House, was Congressman."

"What does all this matter in what you're writing?"

"The Germans' word for 'become' is 'werden.' We derive our word 'worth' from 'Wert' or, if you can get your head around this, something-coming-ahead. The idea is that you can only judge worth backwards, by knowing what it will become, knowing its future. If you see thirst in your future, you value a glass of water. Dick was focused on a bright political future almost to the exclusion of anything else. And his focus was extremely narrow. His focus was shaped by the debating he had done for years in high school, in college and in law school. Political success was that feeling of winning an argument. It was his Great Debate Club, before a huge audience, in which he would be the greatest debater of all time."

"Dick could never, ever argue with one great arguer."

"His father, right. Nothing Frank Nixon liked better than arguing. He was always ready to argue, he loved it, licked it up like a cat at the bowl of milk. Dick warned his brothers about arguing with the old man, but they always did. Only Dick kept his guard, refused to argue with Dad."

"But he wanted to argue."

"In the worst way. It showed outside the house, in debating."

"People say he should never have debated Kennedy."

"People are right. Dick was the known candidate, the Vice President, the familiar face. JFK had no instant recognition going for him, outside of Massachusetts. The debates put him on the map and on the road to victory."

"His face."

"True. The TV audience favored Kennedy, the pretty boy. But those who only heard the debate – the ones listening on radio – were impressed by Nixon the answer boy. Preparation showed. But on TV what showed was baggy eyes, sweat and the guy's five-o'clock shadow."

"Dick Nixon is your Augie March, Gabe. Just hold out your bucket and catch the drops."

CHAPTER THIRTY-FOUR

The rings of Saturn sighted

"I want to be a prong-horn antelope."

"A what elope?"

"A prong-horn antelope," Gabe said, enunciating with exaggerated consonants.

"Why?"

"They have ten times our vision, they can see more clearly than we do. They can see the rings of Saturn."

"Only at night, I bet."

"Of course at night, dummy. But I want to see this meeting between Dick and Pat more sharply than anyone else ever has, and then tell that, describe it," I said. "Conrad said that what he wanted to do as a novelist was to make you see."

"Why do you care? I mean, the rings of Saturn are obvious but why do you care to see Dick and Pat so clearly?"

"Because," I said, with a shrug, "Dick and Pat are us."

"What are you talking about?"

Because Arlene asked, I knew that she had forgotten her own theory. It was she who had discovered our reincarnation. *She* was the one who told *me* days before in this very room. Now, beside my medicine-fogged better half, my duty to lead her to her own knowledge was obvious. So I asked:

"What's your birthday?"

"June 22, 1993."

"When did Pat die?"

"I don't know."

"That day. Your birthday. And I was born on April 22, 1994."

"I know. You're younger than me. That's our constant joke, baby."

"When did Dick die?"

"You're not saying what I think you're saying, are you?"

"Dick died and I was born. I just turned 21."

"We are Dick and Pat reincarnated? That's too weird?"

"Have you ever bought this writer's magazine?"

"No."

"Why did you buy it? For you to read here in the hospital."

"This issue is the one with the Nixon contest."

"It is."

"I would never have picked the topic to write about or research. Or, if I did, I would not follow through. I had to be trapped in the hospital to have time and conditions to focus."

"God made it happen? The accident?"

"He put things in motion to expose the secret to us. Lots of people know about their past lives. You and I didn't. Or did we? Did you ever spend time thinking about Pat Nixon?"

Arlene was suddenly thoughtful and stiffened, her hand came up to her mouth.

"Oh my God," she said. "Third grade. We had a First Lady party and Presidents party. The boys and girls could be anyone they wanted who had been First Lady or President."

"And you picked Pat Nixon?"

"Yes, and so did my best friend, Maxine. And we argued that only one of us could be Pat Nixon but when she told the teacher, Mrs. Brazzil, she said we could both be Pat. So I did Jackie

Kennedy and stopped being Maxine's friend. I never spoke with her again. I hadn't thought of that in years."

"Well," Gabe said. "That's interesting."

"You were Nixon in your third grade Presidents' Day party?"

"No," Gabe said. "My senior thesis, you know, was 'The House Un-American Activities Committee.'"

"So?"

"Its most dramatic episode was the Alger Hiss hearing."

"Starring Richard Nixon?"

"Yes, then a Congressman who was out to earn a name nationally. And did."

"Okay, coincidence. The *DaVinci Code* was not about Richard Nixon."

"You know what year the Committee was established?"

"Don't tell me 1938."

"Then I won't tell you."

"Really?"

"Really. 1938. It could have been the day Dick met Pat that their fated future – all they ever talked or cared about – was coming around the bend at them like a freight train on a track as the Committee was beginning its work in May, 1938."

"But Dick met Pat in January."

"Yeah, right, January or February or any month. January 16th was just the name of the first play he was in, starring as a prosecuting attorney. January 16, 1938, was a Sunday. No day for an audition in Whittier, let alone in a Whittier Church. In Dick's memoirs, he gives no date and implies that it was several months after the beginning of 1938. So the thing is -- which came first, Dick and Pat meeting or HUAC meeting? The chicken or the egg?"

"Tempest in a tea-pot."

"You were Pat Nixon in third grade. I did my thesis on HUAC because when we drew topics out of a hat, that's the topic I got. How about that? And, on a completely subjective note, I thought the index card was electrified, my fingers tingled when I picked it out, and that it glowed when I read it, like a sign."

"You got an A."

"I was there. If I was Dick Nixon, I was there. I was just reviewing my old days."

"So you and I can write this chapter with authority. We were both there."

"We were. Dick and Pat. And that's how come we found each other so compelling when we first met on campus as freshmen at—"

"Oh my God, that's right. Trying out for that play--"

"*You Can't Take It with You*. By George S. Kaufman and Moss Hart, it won the 1937 Pulitzer Prize and was a movie in 1938, revived many times since. Why did you try out?"

"I remembered the movie. Why did you?"

"I wondered if I could speak on stage. I wanted to improve my public speaking ability and fight my stage fright. Plus meet a chick."

"No, really? Meet a chick?"

"I didn't know you were coming. I would have said: to meet *you*."

"But, according to you, Nixon researched and investigated and knew all about Pat before he came into that church that night."

"I'm rethinking. If I did really meet you at my audition in this life and did not know you—"

"This is crazy. Reincarnation isn't real."

"It is."

"Prove it."

"This whole thing is proving it as it unfolds all around us."

"But if you are Dick Nixon, you did a lot of terrible things and I've never thought much of you. And you didn't treat Pat all that well."

"Julie wrote a book how her parents loved one another deeply."

"Gabriel, this cannot be."

"But this perfect, Arle. As you find out, you draw away, just like Pat did. I'm chasing you, I love you but it's not reciprocated."

"It is reciprocated. You stop that. You're not Dick Nixon."

"Since this project began, how many times have you said to me that I was Dick Nixon?"

"Jokingly."

"No, because you saw that I was behaving or talking exactly like Dick Nixon."

"Let's change the subject."

"Okay, Pat."

"Move on."

CHAPTER THIRTY-FIVE

The curious incident

The curious incident in *The Hound of the Baskervilles* was that the dog did not bark. Inexplicably, Dick and Pat never discussed the past. They talked a lot but about the future and the present and weather and nothing in particular, anything and everything but their past. All of the books are full of things Dick and Pat did not talk about or share with one another in Deepest Courtship. Events and people huge in their lives, keys to understanding them, benchmarks in their development, they did not offer up lightly to one another. It was an ongoingly curious series of incidents.

"Arlene, have we told each other about our past?"

"Sure."

"What can you tell me about my past?"

"Well, your grandfather used to tell you kids growing up, if one of you farted, 'Another country heard from,' and you'd all laugh and your mother would tell him, 'Don't say that.'"

"Oh, God," I said. "Anything besides fart jokes?"

"You were in love with Marcia in fourth grade—"

"Mary. Fifth grade."

"And went with her to the Brownies dance."

"Girl Scout dance."

"You used to look for her to sit near on the school-bus in seventh-grade, but it was over. Sorry, Gabe."

"Broke my heart. Yes, you remember. Not names but you remember. I told you."

"What about me?"

"You loved a horse most of your teen-aged years in California, riding the hills. Your first time—"

"Let's leave that be. I told you. I have no desire to hear you tell me."

"Well, it was sweet, anyway. The apple blossoms and when he—"

"Yup, yup. Nothing to see here, move on, please. How about you try and write?"

I agreed. I started.

Although Dick would later, in his memoirs, write of a sixth sense, it was not a sixth sense but a mood that night. On stage, playing free-style, picking out notes with unprecedented abandon on the unfamiliar piano in a room with bad acoustics – nothing to lose – he heard a jazzy, improvised, more rhythmic, full-body tune, altogether offering him a giddiness, an out-of-body sensation of levitation. Dick was in a musician-troubadour-jazzman fit, a grace, death's lightning, free of all restraint, open to the moment. In a hundred years he would be dead. Live now. Really live. Nothing to lose.

Unstoppered champagne, he could dance, kick his heels, speak lines, act intoxicated, be crazy, in love, happy. A wave swept over him that shut down his censor. He was Dionysius in spring, he was an avatar.

When she was in view, he knew what his Dad had known: love at first sight.

He auditioned well. LaDonna was awe-struck. Where had this Dick been?

Dick was the amused and amusing, witty and charming, garrulous and lovable Barry Jones of Broadway. The lawyer with facts at his fingertips and questions on his lips was gone, a changeling in his place who lit up the night. What he had been he was no longer. What was to be had begun. With Pat at his side, they were the king and queen of the moment. It was astonishing. LaDonna never experienced such excitement in a church basement before. It was as if Fat and Free Will struggled and writhed between the lines of the play they were reading, the facile surface of the script and the audible words of that night being as nothing compared to

I stopped.

Incomparable. That night was incomparable. Some days and nights just stand apart.

CHAPTER THIRTY-SIX

If the Accident will

I suppose I always knew that Arlene was not really immune from all illness but for as long as I had known her she had been in more than good health, she had been vibrant, energetic, and lively. It was not that nervous, fidgeting energy of the caffeinated crowd. No, hers was the spilling-over, I've-got-plenty inexhaustible variety of energy, the plasma in the earth's core, the stately progress of the planets in orbit, of the stars in motion. I could not picture Arlene otherwise. My failure, in common with the ordinary defect of the average novelist, was a failure of the imagination.

I noticed her eyes first, even though illness was written all over her body in a sickly pallor, a certain smell of the sick-room, a languor, the smoldering heat of insidious fever, even the splayed-out, played-out posture of her body on the bed. It scared me. No, it really terrified me. And it made all accomplishments I ever achieved trivial in a single stroke: could I do nothing for Arlene now?

"How are you feeling?" I asked.

She turned, it seemed to me painfully, and saw me. It was a person turning to see – what? – an accident. And accident I was, and we were, so unlikely that I stood, the sperm that punctured the egg almost thirty years ago, the old tail-thrashing polliwog up on two legs with seeing eyes, and that I would have met this princess among women, this kind and sweet girl with such a brain. All accident. And now she was ill by the same accident.

Vonnegut said at the beginning of his *Slaughterhouse-Five*, quoting a German cab driver, no less, "If the Accident will," a variant of "as chance will have it."

How was she feeling? You know how she is feeling, you dog. How dare you ask, burden her with having to articulate her suffering – or to lie. To compel Desdemona, for your sake, to say that all was well and you are blameless. How badly I felt to stoop to ask her how she was feeling rather than man up and ask: what can I do for you, dear?

She did not respond but turned away. She did not like stupid questions or bear fools lightly.

"What can I do for you, dear?"

Ah, that was right.

"Sing for me," she said. "Stormy Weather."

Oh, my. That I could do. Not well, but I could do it and I did.

But singing "Stormy Weather" was not all. She asked me to look into her health insurance and I found, within the next twenty-four hours, that she had none. It had expired on June 30, as she had graduated from Harvard. The notice had been on the top of her desk, paper clipped as "To Do." But she had been doing for me instead and she had been too ill and now she was in that awful American nightmare of being very sick and totally uninsured.

I called my father.

Yes, really.

I called my father.

CHAPTER THIRTY-SEVEN

There's still no business like show business

Dick went downstairs and climbed up into his 1935 Chevy. *Brown*. Like a brown tuxedo, it would never be in style. Even Dick wore black shoes, well-polished. He had black hair. The brown car had been left on the lot long enough that it was a bargain. They'd gone all the way to L.A., Don wanted something no more than 5 years old, with new or newish tires, and low mileage. Dick knew that mileage was a matter of opinion and subject to the relative honesty of the sales manager, tires were unpredictable in t6erms of blowing out and that left, within their price range, one 1935 automobile that was brown. Don bitched about that and said he'd paint it himself.

"With what?"

"With a paint brush, of course."

"They don't paint cars with paint brushes, Don."

"I do."

"No, you don't."

With their pooled money, they bought the car -- brown -- on Dick's condition that it stayed brown and Don did not touch it. Brown it stayed, untouched. A small victory on a gas-guzzling, oil-leaking, hard-driven car. But it was a Chevy, and Chevys were pretty reliable cars. Nothing to write home about for style, but "they'll always get you there and back," as the sales guy, a small, hunched-over, wiry smoker said in a rasp between puffs of his Camel. He came with off accessories himself, arms to long that he held before him as if holding an awkward bundle or wanted to hug himself only not in public. "And you guys can afford it," the guy said repeatedly, too, well aware of his major selling point. He may not have known cars, but he knew people. Dick admired that.

Dick in his childhood bed in Yorba Linda had listened to train whistles and thought of faraway places. It pleased his old conductor father, who had a proud photo of himself in uniform when he had driven a streetcar on tracks in Colorado, to hear Dick say that he wanted to grow up to be an engineer. But Dick was not made for an engineer's job. His hands were not the skillful hands of the engine enthusiast. No one was more inept at repairs or on-hands work with machines or, indeed, knives. Dick was excluded from the kitchen, where his younger brother, Don, became the butcher slicing up the meats. Dick was assigned to truck duty, purchasing and preparing produce for the store. The wail of the whistle – the train's *voice* – was what appealed to Dick, the siren call to get underway, to move, to go places. It was his own voice or call to the country that, he felt, would take him places. Not hands on the throttle but the voice of the engineer was his disembodied future hope. The train-whistle. That was what Dick identified with. The train-whistle.

CHAPTER THIRTY-EIGHT

Let me make this perfectly clear

The old maestro deflected attention from himself to his mother on the day of his resignation.

"Nobody will write a book about my mother," was the poignant, pity-evoking, sentimental and cloying lament that he started with. And her ended with the same regret. It was the red cape waved by the bull-fighter at journalists and authors, goading them to charge into writing – about *his mother*. He did not *say* so. He said the *reverse*. But the impact of such a lament, such a regret, especially when he spoke in several sentences about a saint, offered *his mother* up for their analysis and dissection. Find fault in her! You won't, you bastards. My mother was better than your mothers! And always will be! Nyaah-nyaah, nyaah-nyaah. But, oh, no, they'll never write about her the way she deserves whole books, shelves of books, libraries of books, my mother. Oh, no, never. He challenged them, as he resigned in disgrace. Plenty of bitterness to go around.

He said what he wanted to say. He always did.

On September 14, 1955 Dick made a speech to America's connoisseurs of broadcast performances, the Radio and Television Executives Society. At the microphone, leaning forward, almost in a whisper, peek-a-boo to this appreciative audience, three years after the "Checkers" speech that seemed so heart-felt and sincere, the old actor confided, "I want you to be the first to know" --pausing to let it sink in that he *was* an accomplished actor -- "I staged it."

Oh-oh.

If he staged it, then he set Pat up to feel that she was a key when she was not a key, he talked about quitting only to elicit the very response he got from Pat, and he may have had no intention of quitting.

But there was his written, signed resignation the next day. Staged, too? Had Dick fully expected – but taken the Nietzschean Superman come-what-may risk – that Rose Marie Woods would give it to Murray Chotiner and Chotiner would never send it out without either speaking with him first, or that he would (as he did) destroy it without even discussing it with Dick? Putting out a test of their loyalty? Staging a resignation confounded by his loyalists? *Megatheater* in the Vice President's campaign headquarters?

What else was it but acting for the love of acting when Dick, at Duke Law School, wrote unanswered letters so often, so faithfully – love letters – to Ola? He said nothing to anybody around him at Duke about even having a girl back home, he sometimes appeared stag at dances, but he maintained his role as lover. And he continued to enact the role of Ola's lover on stage for almost a year, up to the day of her wedding, when he presented a gift to the couple.

CHAPTER THIRTY-NINE

The End is Near

I hate hospitals, I hate doctors, I hate medicines, I hate the smell, the mixture of unidentifiable stinky sweetness that hits you, the whiff of industrial strength deodorizer that mows down almost – almost – every vestige of poopiness in the place, something of whatever they were cooking, and steam-pipe flavoring, I guess it is. You know you're not home before you open your eyes. It smells like – well, a hospital.

I was sorry for the aroma in the moment that I was finally introducing Arlene and my parents, my mother first, who daintily took Arlene's right hand, ignoring the tubes and very gently, as one might shake a baby's hand, one shake, before placing it down carefully. I thought how she must have been as gentle with me when I had been small.

"Arlene, I'd like you to meet my father," I said, not knowing what to expect.

"Call me Dad," he told Arlene. "We won't disturb you more. I know that you and Gabe will want time together."

It struck me as awkward for Dad to say hello-goodbye that way, not even saying that he was pleased to meet Arlene or to give her any chance to respond, as if her time were so short that this immediate exit was necessary.

"We have time, Dad," I found myself saying. "Don't we, Arlene?"

"Yes," she said. "Sit and join us."

There were, in fact, two chairs. I stood and my parents sat. What should we talk about? I need not have worried, Arlene came through as if she had researched and prioritized topics.

She did not ask how they were, how was their trip, what the weather was. These concessions she made to her limited strength and time. And she did not ask my mother if she could call her Mom, she just did.

"Dad and Mom, I love your son," she said, radiant though pale. "And he loves me."

"Two wonderful people found each other," Mom said. "We're so glad."

"So very glad," Dad added, a man who had not been glad about anything for years.

"Gabe's working on writing a novel. Did you know that?"

My parents said no in chorus.

"He is a gifted author. Your hopes are realized," Arlene said. "He'll be famous before long and reporters will be camped out at your door for interviews, asking about Gabe when he was a child. I wondered what you would tell them. Please."

This could not but be embarrassing, but I was not so boorish as to interrupt or stop this review of my infancy and clever remarks as a child. Arlene prompted the tooth fairy story.

"Did he tell you?" Dad asked, his eyes lighting up to my surprise -- and irritation. Did he actually want to *brag* about it again, like in the old days? He proceeded to tell about the day a tooth fell out, and how I lost it before bed, and cried because the tooth fairy would come and not see it. My father had reassured me that he could deal with this problem. He wrote an affidavit that verified that I had lost a tooth, now lost, for which the Tooth Fairy was directed to pay as if it had been found under my pillow.

"The next morning," my mother said, finishing the story, "Gabe came trotting up to our bed with a dollar and the note, hollering that, 'It worked! It worked!'"

I smiled but Arlene laughed, a happier sound than I'd heard in a few days. Was she possibly feeling better?

Dad was inspired to tell another story about a time I blamed "the little mouse" for having broken a vase in the den, from which I had been under orders to stay out.

"Did we ever find that 'little mouse,' Gabe?"

"No, I don't think we did," I said, telling Arlene, "Our house didn't really have mice. They saw right through my defense."

Arlene said, "Well, you all seem to have good imaginations and I see where Gabe got his start in becoming a novelist. You won't make him become a lawyer, will you?"

"No."

"Promise."

"I promise."

"Cross your heart and hope to die."

"Cross my heart and hope to die."

"Thank you, Dad."

He let fall a tear from each eye.

"Thank you, Arlene," he said, his voice breaking.

"I guess I'm a novelist," I said.

"Think of that," she said. "Can you give us a moment, Mom and Dad?"

They hugged and said good-bye but Arlene told them to wait in the waiting area, that I'd be right along.

"What did you say that for?" I asked.

"Because you, my dear boy, are going to forgive them for everything you ever thought they did wrong."

"I am?" I asked.

One look at her face showed me that I would. She led the way.

We hugged and kissed more intensely than I thought she had strength to hug and kiss. She was like eighty pounds, so light, leaving me. I forced myself not to cry.

"Forgive me, too?" she asked. "For making you forgive everybody for everything?"

"I'm not much of a Nixon," I said. "I think I'm in the forgiveness business."

"My life, my movie," Arlene said.

Then she said she needed to rest, I went out the door, found my parents and we left, all together. Love means never having to say you forgive people.

CHAPTER FORTY

Oh paradise!

> *Jacob: Caruso stands on the ship and looks on a Utopia. You hear? "Oh paradise! Oh paradise on earth! Oh blue sky, oh fragrant air –"*
>
> *— Clifford Odets, "Awake and Sing!"*

The truck farm that her father called a "ranch" smelled always to Pat of highly ammoniac chickens, mingled with bass notes of manure, along with penetrating tangy whiffs of tomatoes and peppers, and the bland, clean wash of lettuce. Not for Pat the scents of flowers, or of cinnamon, as she stood among the different perfumes of ladies on Sunday. In stores a cacophony of raucous, shouting scents tickled her nostrils with new goods smells, effulgent explosions like the leather of a new shoe, luring her to clerk when she could. Even a bank would do. She took flight and found refuge in the smells of money, with its sharp currency-ink smells and slightly sulfurous paper forms. Hollywood stank of stale cigarettes, rank sweat and yeasty beer or sour liquor. Only in night-school at USC, climbing rung by rung up into a merchandising degree did she feel that she was reaching the top of her possibilities, as far from and high over the truck farm as she could possibly reach.

The unexpected offer of a teacher's job in Whittier for one-hundred-and-twenty-five dollars every month interrupted her progress. Smelling citrus fields again during the week, every weekend, without exception, she vacated Whittier for Los Angeles, for her real life, a life from which she would no more be separated that Atlas from the Earth. Perhaps, had the Depression not renewed around, perhaps, had an equally well-paying job at a store been open, perhaps, had she less practicality woven into her upbringing, she might have made a less cautious decision than retreating to Whittier. Her bungalow across from the town's recreation center, a bowling alley, only temporary, she left and kept leaving every Friday. Dick did not want her to take the bus. Dick wanted to drive her to and back. She let him. After a few weeks, oranges came into the picture, the smell.

By May, upon getting into Dick's car, Pat smelled oranges each time. It was Dick. Dick smelled like oranges. This smell of oranges beguiled her with a siren-smellsong of success, of prospering, of selling, of business. Men had mined the hills of California for gold before. Now gold grew on trees in groves and, once peeled, squeezed, packed, frozen, and shipped, it was worth a fortune. Dick was dreaming and going places and that was why Dick smelled like oranges now. He was in the business of making frozen orange juice.

Dick was, thus, the merchandising-major Pat's very own tailor-made Scheherazade with yet another fragment of the ongoing saga of the Prince of Orange in Quest of Fabulous Fortune. Dick tantalized her sense of making money in America through marketing. Dick was onto something needed by everybody every day. It seemed only a matter of time before Dick owned a piece of the breakfast tables of America and siphoned off that portion of the family budgets that was marked off "for orange juice." If he could shift the buying habits of housewives away from the oranges, self-squeezing, or apple juice, and other competitors, with his packages of cheap, delicious frozen orange concentrate, Dick would become wealthy and famous, a real-life "I-knew-him-when" figure in the gallery of Pat's businessmen heroes.

She saw it all unravel, to her horror.

Dick, smelling of oranges, at first a lovely, evocative, nostril-tingling whiff of potential, all unrealized possibilities in the air, sweet and delicious to imbibe, told her about the easy access to oranges, cheap, good quality oranges – he knew, Dick had been the one in his family who took the truck to LA each morning and made the selections and cut the deals at the Seventh Street farmer's market – and the machine that split and squeezed out the juice. It worked perfectly. They were into the stretch, experimenting with packaging, and Dick was investing and helping. On paper, Dick was the president, he was in charge of one of America's newest businesses, and he was at the starting line toward success in the United States. Dick could be the Henry Ford of frozen orange juice. It was all possible at first, and fun to hear about, and she could smell the oranges but her old bank-teller's memory of the smell of money was activated, too. Nobody could sit through as many lectures in as many classes and read as many books on business and on merchandising as Pat without picking up that trail.

But it was coming apart, slowly, in the course of months, the horror of a failing business, despite all of this man's efforts, outside of his law work, nights, weekends, he was telling her about set-backs, impatient investors, complaints, experiments that kept going wrong, when success seemed so close, so certain.

"When do you think it's enough, Pat?"

She shook her head. She wanted to show sympathy but she did not want to slip down the slippery slope, to fall into the rabbit-hole of quitting, or to suggest or approve or countenance Dick's quitting. Persevere, do it, keep agoing, never say die, was bred into her bones.

"I think I've had enough."

Pat shook her head, she looked down the road, they were on the way to LA again on Friday, where he would drop her off at her sister, Neva's, house and where she would go out on the town with some far less interesting, glib man, a man who would seem a boy without a story compared to Dick, who smelled of oranges.

Dick, you see, was rising. Dick worked. He knew no leisure. Dick was not lying around on the beach. Pat was his equal, the one he needed to certify him as Somebody and not Anybody Anyplace. Pat was the first of them, anyway. If she knew him really well and still received him, then millions would follow. Pat was the test Dick had to pass.

CHAPTER FORTY-ONE

Loneliness after midnight

"You know what reincarnation is? Really?"

"Tell me, Arle. I'm all ears."

"The Buddha in me, the same as in all of us, is oozing Buddhas from out of every pore, and those Buddhas are oozing Buddhas, a universe of Buddhas, at every moment, and creating the universe, my words, too, are striking your ears and rolling around in there, curly-top, and coming up with new stuff, stuff I never even thought of. That won't stop, that won't ever stop."

"No."

"If I stop breathing, if my heart stops, my body will begin to change and fall to pieces of something new, and I might serve for a tree root, and grow to life again. Ya think, honey?"

"I think," I said, by now my cheeks were wet. I was becoming water.

"The bugle notes, I hear. And I know we have a future. We've been Tristan and Isolde, Antony and Cleopatra, Dick and Pat, Gabe and Arlene and we'll be more. This love will never die."

"No."

"My life, my movie."

"Sure is."

"Don't forget me."

"Couldn't if I tried."

"I'll always be with you."

"We're a couple."

"We are. We're a couple."

"Brats."

"Not any more. We broke through. Brats no more."

I bent over and we kissed one of those gentle kisses that Bret Harte said you could hear over the breeze in the pine trees in California. She looked beautiful, innocent and radiant.

Dr. Patel came in because a monitor alarm was going off. We hadn't heard it, too wrapped up talking, listening to bugle notes. I stepped aside to let him and a team of several who rushed in all in a hurry, all at once to try and save the body of Arlene Rzeczny from losing its grip on her immortal soul but Arlene was too quick for them. She had been ready for a while. It was her sweetness to stay long enough, for my sake, to wish me and to kiss me goodbye.

CHAPTER FORTY-TWO

I Won't Dance, Don't Ask Me

Arlene and I shared so many things that it is not possible to single out one as more important than another. I remember her getting me a glass of water in the hospital, I'm glad the drugs did not eat the memory. I suppose it was nothing special but for me it was because it was Arlene. Another thing, before she got really sick, Arlene looked up Theodosia Filbert, who founded the contest.

"She died young. Young and rich, from a start-up search engine company, sort of a Facebook for former lives. Your friends are all people you used to be, supposedly."

"Did anybody believe that?" I asked.

"Only two million subscribers," Arlene said.

"Big in California, huh?" I asked rhetorically. She continued, undistracted, of course. That was my Arlene.

"Theodosia bequeathed the contest in her will. And I found one more thing," my then-indefatigable Arlene said.

"Yes?" I asked. "Tell me."

"Theodosia was born on September 18, 1969."

"So she died young. You already said so," I said.

"That's not my point," my chief researcher said, sounding fresh, as if I was too slow by her standards.

"What is your point then, beloved angel?"

"LaDonna Baldwin died that same day in a nursing home in Arizona."

After a moment of shock, I said, "So you think, you're saying, suggesting that this Theodosia our benefactor was LaDonna Baldwin reincarnated?"

"Seems like. Gabe, you remember telling me that you were born on the day Nixon died?"

"Yes, it always seemed a strange fact," I said. "Stranger now, I suppose."

"Do you know when I was born?"

I rattled off the date, worried where this was leading.

"Do you know what else happened that day?"

"No," I said, not "no" as in I didn't know but "no" as in "Don't tell me, no, please, no."

She told me: it was the same day that Pat died.

There we sat, Arlene and I, mulling over these facts, these coincidences.

"What are you thinking?" I asked.

She looked up at me, saying that in searching Theodosia's website – she had become a free trial subscriber for a month -- connections or links between Theodosia and a once-famous cult figure in the spiritualist movement kept popping up, a Frenchman who devoted himself especially to a study of one phenomenon: recovering past lives of the reincarnated. She told me her idea.

"If we could find a book, a manuscript on reincarnation, likely in handwriting, likely in French, about 150 to 200 years old, in among the rest of Theodosia's papers, it might be a breakthrough. Her papers are archived at Stanford but they're not yet accessed, there are no finding aids. Nobody's opened the boxes since she died."

"Falling in love in this life is the only happiness we need," I said, but I sounded lame in my own ears.

"We'll live on the sidelines and hurt nobody," she said, dreamily. "But I still want to look."

I said, "I don't want to spend the rest of our lives spreading the word about reincarnation, or trying to that book."

"No big search, Gabe. It's in California at Stanford."

"Then you check on it. You're the research assistant," I said, knowing that if she went, I'd go, too, and face the Frenchman.

That's as far as it got. Arlene never did check on it. She got sick and we never did go out to California. I outlived her. And I wrote about my love, our love, and Dick Nixon frighteningly in love, too. In love, at least, when he did not fear that he was not serious. That part still gets me every time. That guy.

CHAPTER FORTY-THREE

Heading for home

Disconcerted, even distraught, as he drove the car, alone at the wheel, downshifting gears and proceeding slowly, Dick thought about her, who was she. Words stopped seething in his head. In an underwater, wombish silence, informed only by his heartbeat, images of a beautiful face, her eyes on him, their encounter – so puzzling to him rationally but flashes of images he now, without exercising judgment, saw all in passing – buzzing and fizzing in the center of his stomach. At Dick's right at the horizon of the great Pacific the sun was setting, seeping, weeping, achingly beautiful bright red, purple, golden, colors urging his attention, attention Dick denied them. Above him, unseen, clouds were adrift and more than half-covered the skies. He drove forward in this lighted moment of the ineffable, a time outside of human speech, into the future, a future together.

After parking, Dick was almost levitating, dizzy, he had to stop a moment before placing his hand upon the cool brass knob of the basement door. The light was on already over the door, although it was not yet dark. *Dad would have given them hell for wasting "current."*

As he stood before the church, everything white, white and black, Dick felt light-headed, woozy, seeing, imagining images, faint and faraway, hallucinations, and feeling elated, feeling happy, feeling angry, and feeling sad as some distant bugle blew. *Dada-da-dee-dada-dee.* Patton. *Was that not the name? The movie about the General who—in which war? World War Two? How?* Dick broke off fumbling for any further clarity and marched forward, one foot in front of the other until he opened the door and went in, although still haunted, unable to shake some sort of monster mind with pieces that remained himself and pieces from another being, a fantasy self, a creation that knew, somehow "knew" by a sixth sense was real. *World War Two, Navy service in the Pacific, a flash of fright, debating against Kennedy. President Kennedy. What? Then that movie, again.* Patton. *Most definitely,* Patton. *Distant bugles on an old battlefield, General Patton was there, in a past life. A color movie. The American flag and the General. "All real Americans love a good fight," in a gravelly voice. It was coming to him.* Patton. *It was his favorite movie.*

"Dick," a voice said.

"Oh, LaDonna," Dick said, offering his hand.

LaDonna well knew not to hug Dick. She shook his hand with decorous brevity and at a proper distance, standing just as stiffly as he did.

"I'm very glad to see you. I was worried about casting the male roles but now that you're here, I'm relieved."

Liar. If that were true, LaDonna Liar, then why didn't you call and invite me? Dick thought. *Earlier, this past year, LaDonna had called him, asking Dick to try out for her Ayn Rand play. He thought he'd done a great job as the prosecutor in that production. The newspaper thought so, too. And LaDonna had said something to him about "brilliant" and "a wonderful performance" afterwards, at the cast party. Words, words, words. People lie. She may not have thought so highly at all of his demonstrated histrionic ability. At least, she had not called him for this one.*

Both hands went up to his forehead as Dick bowed under a rush of incoming thoughts. *What was this? Who? Whit Chambers? Hiss? HUAC? Papers in a pumpkin, a hearing in a hotel room. A young, skinny guy at the Los Angeles Biltmore accepting the nomination for President. What was the speech Dick himself was giving, sitting in front of a camera with – her name was Pat. Pat. Pat was his wife. His wife.*

"You look tired, Dick," LaDonna said. "If you feel dizzy, why not sit down?"

"I do. I will," Dick said, accidentally reciting a key line in *Henry IV, Part 2*, when Henry V banishes Falstaff. The moment that the prince became the King.

LaDonna slipped Dick a script before he shakily took a seat on one of the folding chairs on the left side of the last row. He always preferred aisle seats.

In a few minutes, his mind cleared. Finally solemn, serious, sad again, Dick looked down at the script. Yet the seizure or whatever was not yet over. Much less clearly, vaguely playing in background, faint pseudo-memories, little scenes, crazy, imaginative movies had not released him from their hold. What was he seeing -- or imagining – was it his future? Dick was always imagining a future, certainly, but never so vividly and confusingly as tonight. Tonight, he was possessed by a sort of fever dream. He hallucinated raising his hand and swearing on oath to preserve, protect and defend the Constitution of the United States.

So help me God, he thought*, this is insane. Am I going crazy?*

Then Dick felt Pat near, in waves, like shot-wave signals, something, nothing, static, wildly erratic, possibly indoors, outdoors, or in a car (*his car? his brown Chevy? tan upholstery?*) and he somehow perceived Pat's coltishness, her jumpiness, he sensed a woman imminently resisting being tagged by any man. *But I'm not just any man,* he thought, *I'm not, I'm not.* Fleetingly but audibly, he heard a voice like his own in passing: *I am not a crook.* Then Pat was back, Pat, upon first meeting him, Pat bolting. Why, Pat? Some scene with Pat, holding her, came but soon faded. He was back in the basement, in this church that was not his, auditioning for a play that they might perform together. Pat. *Sure,* his sixth sense said: *be ready for Pat, the girl you're going to marry.*

Time resumed.

In through the doorway came two women. He knew Elizabeth Cluett but the tall and slender, auburn-curled beauty with such high cheekbones beside Liz was new to him.

Pat?

My love?

Can you ever forgive me?

CHAPTER FORTY-FOUR

No more

I looked over my options, the several chapters I had written and could submit, but the enthusiasm I once had felt had passed quietly away along with Arlene. I submitted nothing to the contest. I wrote instead about loving Arlene, about my accident, and the contest, our research, Nixon in love, especially his love of the Sound Mirror. Don't forget the magnetic tape recorder invented by Semi Begun, first commercially available through the Brush Development Company of Cleveland, a killer if ever there was one, speak into it and die, Dick, or live forever in the soundrooms of National Archives heaven. Bah. When I was done, when I had finished this whole mass of pages, I gathered everything up and formatted it with a cover and posted it as a novel online instead. Yes I said yes I will Yes.

By the way, I don't know who won the contest, or if anybody did. You check that out yourself, if you're interested. There is no past, no future, everything flows in an eternal present. (James Joyce, no fool, is saying that even now.)

Here and now, I only know that I met and I loved my soulmate for as long as we had together and that, during that whole blessed time, I didn't really know about reincarnation, God help me, but however much we beat on against the current, we were borne back into the past, back to Dick and Pat and the Saint Matthias Church and 1938, which were and are and will be forever swirling and misting and stirring above American waters.

"Don't let it end like this. Tell them I said something." (Pancho Villa).

Huh?

Printed in the United States
By Bookmasters